OF DESIRE

DAVID HELWIG

VIKING

VIKING
Published by the Penguin Group
Penguin Books Canada Ltd, 2801 John Street, Markham, Ontario,
Canada L3R 1B4
Penguin Books Ltd, 27 Wrights Lane, London W8 5TZ, England
Viking Penguin Inc., 40 West 23rd Street, New York, New York 10010,
USA
Penguin Books Australia Ltd, Ringwood, Victoria, Australia
Penguin Books (NZ) Ltd, 182-190 Wairau Road, Auckland 10,
New Zealand

Penguin Books Ltd, Registered Offices: Harmondsworth, Middlesex,
England

First published 1990

1 3 5 7 9 10 8 6 4 2

Copyright © David Helwig, 1990

*Publisher's note: This book is a work of fiction. Names, characters, places
and incidents either are the product of the author's imagination or are used
fictitiously, and any resemblance to actual persons living or dead, events, or
locales is entirely coincidental.*

Printed and bound in Canada on acid free paper ∞

Canadian Cataloguing in Publication Data
Helwig, David, 1938-
Of desire

ISBN 0-670-82592-1

I. Title.

PS8515.E48046 1990   C813'.54   C89-095242-6
PR9199.3.H435046 1990

American Library of Congress
Cataloguing in Publication Data Available
0-670-82592-1 OF DESIRE 89-51998

OF DESIRE

1

"He may be alive or he may be dead," Arnold said. "There's no way of knowing."

"Are you going out there?" Donald said.

"One of us should."

"Better you than me."

Arnold picked up his glass from the coffee-table and drained it.

"Do you want another?"

His brother nodded. Arnold carried the glasses to the kitchen. Ice from the small plastic bucket in the freezer. He poured large unmeasured shots over the mist-coloured cubes and watched them float up.

"How long till you get your licence back?" he said as he handed Donald the drink.

"Six months. I just drive without it."

Arnold sipped his drink. Donald's stocky body was bent double in the chair, one leg thrown over the arm. His jacket, an ancient suede with wide pockets, was

tossed over the back of the chair, and his head was
resting on it.

"Why do we always do this late at night?" Arnold
said.

"This?"

"You and I, Donald, sitting here talking."

"It was always late at night we talked. Upstairs by
ourselves."

"And they were downstairs."

"She was," Donald said.

"But earlier on."

"I don't remember."

"You were ten."

"I remember that mother was downstairs. Except
for the times when she stayed in bed for days."

"She never made a sound down there."

"You told me that if I listened hard enough I'd hear
her turning the pages of her book."

"Did I?"

"Every night I'd lie there trying to hear. I'd strain so
hard that I'd hear all kinds of noises in my ears. It
made me dizzy."

"My room was closer to the stairs."

"I think it was just something you told me. You
never thought I might take it seriously."

"I don't remember saying it."

"Probably it was just something you said to get me
out of your room."

"Perhaps I believed it."

"You just said it to get rid of me."

"Are you holding a grudge about it?"

"I got used to those things."

"What things?"

"Being outsmarted."

"Were you?"

"Most of the time. Always one step back, trying to catch up."

"You were younger."

"I could never find out what was going on."

"Didn't you ask?"

"No. I knew that you wouldn't tell me the truth, any of you."

"As if we knew the truth. Any of us."

"Everybody thought I was too young and stupid to understand. And I was. Lying there trying to hear the pages of mother's book turning. Pathetic."

"I was probably trying to comfort you when I told you that."

"Probably."

"It wasn't malicious."

"You handled me."

"Sometimes. You were five years younger."

"You used to slip out of the house at night. After she'd turned out the lights."

"Yes."

"You wouldn't tell me where you went."

"No."

"Secrets. There were always secrets."

"I was fifteen or sixteen. I needed to have secrets."

"What did you do when you went out all those nights?"

"It was kind of a game. I was Master of the Night City."

"What?"

"That's what I called myself when I went out. I explored back lanes and obscure little streets and alleys. I'd find an old chair on somebody's front porch, and I'd take it and leave it on another front porch a block away. Or I'd put a rake and shovel in the wrong yard. If I found a bicycle unlocked, I'd ride it for a while and put it someplace strange, hanging on a fence or in a tree. Sometimes if I saw lights on, I'd look in windows. I liked to feel that I knew everything about everyone, that I was a mysterious, solitary figure. I was Master of the Night City."

Arnold got up from his chair and crossed to the leaded windows at the front of the apartment. Beyond his brother's figure, Donald could see over the rooftops to the lights blinking on the CN Tower and the patches of brightness at the windows of apartment and office towers. Tall shining properties, respectable, good as gold. The figure of his older brother was slender, dressed in a light sweater and a pair of dark blue pants, leather slippers. There was a bald patch at the back of his head. There was a stillness about him, a quietness that Donald had always envied.

"You could have told me about that," he said.

"No," Arnold said, without turning back. "It would have spoiled it. I needed to have some powerful secret."

"Did you ever tell anyone?"

"Marie. Years later."

"Did you look in windows at women?"

"When I could."

"A Peeping Tom."

"It gave me a sense of power over the people I watched. That's why I called myself by that name. I knew secrets. I had forbidden knowledge."

"Why are you telling me all this?"

"You asked."

"I thought you went to visit *him*."

"Sometimes I went by their house."

"Did you look in the windows?"

"No."

"I don't believe you."

Arnold turned away from the window and returned to his chair. Even a small lie brought its load of
weariness. He studied the two Chinese scrolls on the
wall beside him, one a landscape, an eighteenth-
century ink drawing, and the other a poem by Wang
Wei written by a celebrated calligrapher. His
daughter's friend Elena had spoken of coming back
sometime to see them again. He imagined her fine
long fingers curved around one of the blue and white
Chinese tea bowls.

"You still happy enough here?" Donald said.

"Yes. I like the apartment. Isn't it time you raised
my rent?"

"I soak the other people in the building to cover it."

"What about rent controls?"

"I predicted they were coming and cranked up all
my rents ahead of time. That and the percentage your
government will allow me carries the place," Donald
said.

"Not my government."

"You work for them."

"Not in rent control."

"You would if they sent you there."

"I've been around a long time. I can pick and
choose. They don't send me places I don't want to
go."

"You just have to fill in your time till retirement."

"You could put it that way."

"You once told me you wanted a safe place so
you'd have the freedom to write your poems."

"I suppose that's the way I planned it. Then the
poems stopped coming."

"Just those two books."

"And all the government reports. Probably a dozen
books if you count those."

Donald sipped his whisky. There was a coldness in his brain, and something grey, vertiginous. Little icy-footed mice were running through the spaces between his thoughts.

"I bought a couple more houses this afternoon," he said.

"Did you get a good deal?"

"Have to wait and see."

"You're not often wrong."

"That's why I think you should invest your money with me instead of with that trust company."

"We're brothers. Money and investment, those are something different."

"You think my business has no class."

"I've never said that."

"You're probably right. I do things that would disgust you."

"Do you?"

"I rent places to disgusting people. You have to deal with them at their own level."

"That's probably true."

"The only time it bothers me . . . it never bothers me."

"It bothers you when you imagine mother knowing what you're doing."

"You've turned out the way she'd like, Arnold."

"She'd be glad to see you succeed."

"What would she think if she knew that every penny I got went into crappy old houses, mortgaged as high as I could get them, full of drunks and perverts."

"You talk yourself down, Donald. Some of them are in good neighbourhoods. This is a fine apartment building."

"Some of those places, you could paper the walls

with the work orders against them."

"You take pride in it."

"You bring it out in me. You're so orderly. Meticulous."

"You've always wanted to believe that I was good and boring, and you were bad and adventurous."

"It was the only way I could compete with you. On your own territory, you were invulnerable."

"I seemed so to you."

"Mother thought you were perfect."

Donald took the wide crystal highball glass from the table and stared into it, then drank with an abrupt motion.

"So you think he's dead?" Donald said.

"Yes."

"I don't believe it."

"Men of seventy-nine don't usually run away from home."

"You think he's in the water."

"It's the only thing that makes sense."

"He wouldn't kill himself."

"Why not?"

"He wasn't the type."

"You haven't seen him for years. He might have been depressed."

"If he was, he'd have made someone else pay for it, wouldn't he?"

"Maybe Sandra."

"I hope so."

"You still blame her."

"I blame them both for what they did to mother."

"These things happen, Donald. Marriages break up."

"People who don't want to stay married shouldn't get married. If he wanted to screw Sandra, he could have found a discreet way to do it without ruining his marriage."

"I suppose he thought he was in love."

"Horseshit. That kind of love is horseshit."

Arnold didn't answer.

"So you're going to go out there?"

"I have a flight to Vancouver."

"Have you seen her recently?"

"Sandra? No."

"Do you suppose she's spent all his money?"

"I doubt it."

Donald sipped the whisky in his glass and looked over the shining rim at his brother. No matter what outrageous things Donald said or did, he could never get through to Arnold. The face was calm, perhaps a little melancholy, but wholly under control. It was a good-looking face in a still, pale way, evenly featured, perfectly oval.

"Why is it," Donald said, "I never know anything about you? You're so private."

"You know about me."

"No. Not really. You're like him. You don't give anything away."

"If you want to know something, ask."

"You had a woman since Marie died?"

"No."

"You tell me, but you don't tell me."

"We're different. When I tell you things, you don't hear them."

"Or hear them and don't believe them."

"Still, I'm glad you come round."

"Tell me about your poetry, why you're not writing."

"I am, a few lines, just recently."

"Does anyone remember the other books?"

"Some people. I'm in a couple of the reference books."

"You should have been born in some other century, Arnold."

Donald tossed back the last of the whisky in his glass and stood up, looking across to where his brother sat, his long body held neatly upright in his chair, his feet on the small white rug that interrupted the shining pattern of the parquet floor.

"I'll see you when you get back," he said.

"Drive carefully for once. If they stop you tonight, you'll end up in jail."

"That's probably where I belong."

"No," Arnold said, "you wouldn't like it."

"What do you know about jail?"

"Don't you remember? I worked for the Solicitor-General. Years ago."

"I'd forgotten."

"I've worked in so many ministries, I find it hard to remember myself."

Donald waved from the door and went out. Arnold didn't move after the door was closed, only sat and looked at the scrolls. He and Marie had bought them at an auction at the Christie's gallery in South Kensington many years before. The written scroll recorded a quatrain by Wang Wei, one from the Wang river sequence, an autumn poem about endless sadness.

Arnold stood up and walked to the window. They were solitary figures, those old Chinese poets, catching at moments of joy or friendship or sorrow. A car moved in the street below him, the lights of an apartment building across the street were turned on. The city was full of men and women living their lives. The ancient poem of Wang Wei hung in its place behind him.

Donald was driving west. He tilted the seat of the white Buick Park Lane and drove with one hand, his other draped over the back of the passenger seat. Ahead of him a light turned yellow, but he stepped down, and the eight-cylinder engine accelerated quickly and quietly as he ran the light. He was driving west on Dupont to take another look at the houses he'd bought that afternoon. The deal wouldn't close for a month, but he couldn't see any problems. The same family had owned them for thirty years, so there might be some ancient complications with the title, but he didn't expect it. The neighbourhood wasn't much, but he could break both houses into apartments that would carry the investment, and he figured that in four or five years prices in that area would take off. It was just a matter of being ahead of the market and not wasting money on them in the meantime. He could knock up the partitions himself, and he knew plumbers and electricians who didn't charge for more than they did. Nothing was cheap, but the houses hadn't been rented before so he could get a good price for them without the rent control office climbing down his throat.

It was a game, creeps trying to skip out on their rent, lawyers and real-estate agents out to get their percentage, the building inspectors spying on him, looking for a missing soffit, a broken stair rail, anything that would allow them to send another work order and justify their existence, while the politicians used rent control to buy tenant votes by chopping his percentage wherever they could. It was a game, and you had to be quick. Donald was. There were easier investments, but if he stayed with houses, it was partly because he liked the dance.

He pulled up across the road from the two houses, shut off the engine and sat there studying them. There was a real-estate agent's sign on the lawn, with a Sold sticker pasted on. In fact the sign had arrived only after the houses were sold. The listing agent had given Donald a call and he'd bought the two houses before they were advertised. One had a covered front porch, the edge of it sloping toward the ground where the supports were broken. He could slide a couple of concrete blocks under it. The porch of the other had been torn off. Inside they were identical, and he'd treat them the same way. Build a partition at the foot of the stairs to separate the two apartments. There was a pantry off the kitchen of each where he could put a small bathroom.

In a month the houses would be his.

When he got home, the house was dark. Daphne had gone to bed. He liked entering the house in the dark, finding his way to the bedroom without turning on any lights, treading silently, dropping his clothes to the floor and sliding between the covers to find his wife's big warm body beside him. He put his hand out slowly and touched the cotton nightgown, then followed the shape of her body until he discovered the bare flesh of her knee. His hand moved under the fabric and caressed her, his body moving towards hers. She moaned a little, half-waking, and he moved on top of her. She was hot and soft, and when he was inside her, he pushed the nightgown up until her breasts were big in his hands. At first she was passive and still, but gradually she began to move with him, something powerful and hidden rocking him, swallowing him. They could spend half the night like this.

Awake now, she pulled off the nightgown that bunched at her neck, and her arms and legs closed round him.

"I bought us two more houses," he whispered in her ear.

She turned her head, and their mouths met.

"You taste of whisky," she said.

"Arnold was feeding me Scotch."

She was drawing him further and further into her belly, her flesh moving in waves against his.

2

Behind, to the east, was a ghost mountain, a pale white peak in a haze of sky. It would disappear momentarily and then the eye would catch it again. A single sharp snow-covered peak, the shadows blue, the same clear blue as the sky, so that the white outline might have been wisps of cloud, or something sketched on the sky by the merest hint of desire.

The sound of the world was heavy against his ears, the loud wind that ruffled the surface of the strait, the pounding of the ferry's engine, the splashing of water against the hull. The wind was so strong that to cross the deck, he had to cling to the wall of the forward cabin and keep one hand on the white metal rail. Inside the high sloping cabin windows, a woman and child watched his passage, the odd tilt of his body, his thinning hair tossed about by the wind.

The air was cold, and the late afternoon sun burned against the skin of his face, made him squint, but he couldn't bring himself to return to one of the inside cabins. He had stood out here ever since they had left the dock. At first the Gulf Islands had been only mountainous shapes against the sky and water, their edges softened by mist, but now the ferry was in the narrow passage between Galiano and Mayne and the island shapes were articulated in hillsides of evergreens.

There was something about this landscape that made him aware they were pointed toward the Far East. Something in the purity of line that was abstract, oriental; a landscape haunted by mountains, shaped by mist. He stared down at the metallic green of the water, where the sunlight was fragmented by the multiple reflecting surfaces. Ahead of the ferry and to one side, he saw a black form; it slipped under the water and then appeared again. It was a seal, observing the boat passing by. It dived and reappeared and dived again and was gone.

A messenger from the dark places under the sea. They had been coming at him lately, these messages, images overloaded with some mysterious weight of immanence. The brainstorm that was poetry. And travel did it to him, a mild derangement that made the world thicker, more rough-textured. He travelled too little.

It was only this morning that his daughter Julia had driven him to the airport in Toronto. Since he didn't know how long he'd be away, he'd left the car with her. His plane had followed the sun across the sky to Vancouver, and almost from the moment of take-off, the blood in his brain was quick. Perhaps it was the artificial pressure in the cabin, or the enforced stillness, or the confusion of the body's clock, but he couldn't stop noticing things: a native family at the

Vancouver bus terminal, the father grossly fat, the mother bone thin; the early flowers in the streets; the soft, rubbly texture of the ploughed garden lands of the Fraser delta.

Arnold wanted to write a letter, to capture it all, but there was no one to write to. Marie was gone, Julia too close and too strange. It was Elena he wanted to write to, foolishly, but he didn't know her address, and besides he hardly knew her, and she was young enough to be his daughter, was his daughter's friend.

She was his daughter's friend, but she was someone else, the Elena he had met in the museum, among the Chinese artifacts, both of them studying the heavenly horse. The ancient Chinese said of these horses that they sweated blood, that they were, in fact, dragons.

The ferry blew its horn loudly, another noise crowding his head along with all the others. Soon they'd come in sight of Saltspring and Vancouver Island itself. He was approaching his father. Or his father's ghost. As for his father's body, it might be anywhere, might be tossing in the turbulence created by this ferry. The seal might be his messenger.

The dead sent no messages. Not any more. They hadn't learned how to tune themselves in on semiconductors. Electrons spoke only in the present tense, perhaps the future. Only poets and scholars sighed for the old sentimentality of the pluperfect.

And was the man dead? Maybe Donald was right, and this was just some bizarre trick, a refusal to rot silently away into old age. He tried to recall Sandra's voice on the phone. She had been controlled, factual. What else to be?

When the ferry arrived at the dock, Arnold walked off and made his way to the front of the terminal to pick up his bag, then stood by the door looking for a cab. The evening air was fresh, cool, watery, and the branches of the tall evergreens moved in a light breeze. A kind of spruce? B.C. fir? The light, the shape of the land and water, the colour of the trees, they were all unexpected, unaccountable. This was an island in the Pacific. This was some other kingdom.

Arnold asked the cab driver to find him a motel not too far from the house that was his ultimate destination. Once checked into a room, he unpacked his clothes, shook out the wrinkles, hung them up, then dialled the number of his father's house: Sandra's house.

"Hello." He didn't recognize the voice. Wondered if he'd dialled the wrong number.

"Is Sandra Riggs there please?"

There was a momentary pause.

"Well," the voice said, "she is. But the fact is, she's sleeping."

"Would you tell her that Arnold Riggs phoned."

"Oh," the voice said. "She said you might call. You're Ross's son, aren't you?"

"Yes."

"I'm Stephanie. We live next door, Bill and I, and we've been watching over her a bit since Ross . . . I just got her to take a sleeping pill. I think it's better that she sleeps, don't you?"

The woman sounded nervous and uncomfortable, as if she weren't used to making decisions for other people and expected that taking this kind of responsibility would get her in trouble sooner or later.

"I think it's much the best thing to let her sleep," Arnold said.

"Yes," the woman said, "I think so."

"Would you tell her that I'll come by about eleven

tomorrow morning?"

"Yes. I will."

"Thank you."

"But what about you?" the woman said abruptly. "Don't you need a place to stay? I mean you're right here, on the island, aren't you? Sandra said you were coming. You could stay with us, with Bill and I," she said. "We have an extra room."

"I found a motel," Arnold said. "I'm fine. Just tell Sandra I'll come by in the morning. Around eleven."

After he hung up the phone, Arnold went and lay down on the bed, his hands behind his head. He was filed for the night in this clean, functional room. He was visible, perhaps, to no one on earth, oh, momentarily to Stephanie Whoever, who would be writing a note to Sandra before returning across the lawn to her own house. It was unlikely that Julia would cast a thought in his direction while she worked on her puppets, those odd cloth and wood companions, though he might pass through Donald's mind, that intricate, ill-lit junk-shop of a mind. Might a thought of him cross Elena's mind? Or the mind of Lydia Malcovitch, his secretary? Possible, such things were possible, but it was far more likely that he existed only for himself, at this moment, in this plain room.

In this other kingdom, ocean and rainforest, rock and Douglas fir.

On the table beside him lay two books, the Penguin *Poems of the Late T'ang* and a recent biography of Robert Lowell, along with a paper on possible changes in government policy toward provincial archival materials which he had brought with him from his office. He picked up none of them. His body was still throbbing with the resonance of the ferry engines, his mind glittering with sunlight on the water. Once again he

began to feel that he was in the grip of something that
might be or become poetry yet wouldn't clothe itself
in words. He had become mute, and words came only
if they were coldly willed. Yet there was something
that sought expression. He was like a wife who longs
for love and yet goes rigid at her husband's touch.

Somewhere, not far away, blanked by drugs, Sandra
slept alone in the house she had shared with his
father. Was she prostrated by grief and guilt? While
Marie was alive, they had visited from time to time,
but since her death, Arnold had contented himself
with letters at Christmas and on his father's birthday,
letters that his father answered in kind, with cool
aplomb. Arnold had come to deal with him as he
might have with an old and influential politician,
discreetly and with good manners that stopped short
of servility.

He was not unfeeling, he told himself, only a little
afflicted with worldliness. A career in the civil service,
a lifetime of infinite adaptability had made him an
ironist. Or perhaps it went back even further. As an
adolescent he had wandered secretly about the city, an
observer even then.

Now he was here to mourn. He couldn't imagine
that his father was still alive. Donald saw him, had
always seen him, as a powerful figure instinct with
magic, but that was, Arnold was sure, mostly projec-
tion. Their father was a man, and mortal.

Arnold tried to think of something about his father
that he could mourn. Perhaps he had grieved over his
loss long ago, when he had abandoned them for
Sandra, or when he had moved west. Arnold had
liked the man, and yet he felt about him only the
sense of loss one might feel for a distant uncle, an old
friend of the family.

He might, he supposed, have regarded this as some failing, some emotional paralysis in his own nature. Didn't. A puzzling thing, emotion, disobedient to the call of convention and propriety, flowing from its own springs and along its own path, the areas of rich ferny growth and dry rock arbitrary and miraculous.

Arnold sat on the edge of the dock and looked across the water to where the small shape of the motorboat turned toward the far shore of the lake. Behind it, his brother Donald leaned outward and guided his water skis over the choppy waves of the boat's wake. The sun was hot on his back as he sat there, and he was nervously aware of Sandra, his father's new wife, sitting in a wicker chair on the dock behind him.

"Are you going to the dance tonight?" she said.

"I thought I might."

The boat had disappeared behind one of the islands near the far shore.

"Are you going to go out on the skis?" Sandra said.

"Not today. What about you?"

"No."

"Why not?"

"I'd make a fool of myself. I don't want you watching me fall off."

"Dad said you're pretty good."

"Better than I was at the beginning of the summer, but I'm not as good as you and Donald. I don't want you laughing at me."

Arnold turned around to look at her. She put down her magazine, and her eyes met his as he turned.

"I wouldn't laugh at you," he said.

"No, you wouldn't, would you. But Donald would."

"He's twelve. What's it matter?"

Sandra stood up from her chair and walked to the edge of the dock. She stepped gingerly over the hot wood, then stood looking out over the water. She had long slender legs. In the distance, they could hear the buzzing of the boat's motor, but otherwise the air was still, except for a soft lapping of waves against the boat-house nearby. Arnold was too aware of her bare legs and arms, the curve of her thighs. When she was dressed, Sandra looked thin, but in a bathing suit, you could see the shape of her breasts. She looked toward him, the blue eyes and straight mouth giving her face a composed look.

"I'd like to go dancing some night," she said.

"I'm taking the canoe," he said. "You could take the motorboat."

"I don't think Ross would want to go."

Arnold wondered for a second if she might be saying she wanted him to take her to the dance.

She dived into the water, a neat dive, her knees lightly flexed and then a quick push off with her feet, her toes pointed as her body sliced into the water. Arnold remembered coming here with his mother, when his parents were still married, how she would sit at the top of the hill to watch them. The water frightened her.

Sandra was swimming back to the dock. She came round to the shallow side to climb on, and as she lifted her leg for the high step up, he saw a curl of her pubic hair at the edge of the bathing suit, dark against the pale skin.

"Going in?" she said, giving him a push with her wet hands.

"Don't push," he said and got to his feet.

"Why not?" she said and shoved him toward the water. The hair was matted against her head, and she was grinning at him. She reached out to push him again.

"Cut it out," he said, and grabbed her to hold her off. They were gripping each other by the arms, and she was trying to wrestle him toward the edge of the dock. Arnold was surprised how strong she was, and he had to fight back to keep from being pushed in the water. He was starting to get an erection, and in his bathing suit it would be obvious. He pulled away from her, turned and dived. He came to the surface and observed her on the dock towelling her hair. He heard the motorboat coming closer now. Probably Donald was going to pass the dock and drop one ski.

Arnold turned his body, dived under, and swam downward toward the bottom. The water was deep here, and he had to force himself down, his head and chest feeling the pressure of the depth, his arms and legs struggling to carry him toward the bottom. He touched. Almost out of breath, he looked toward the oily patch of sunlight at the surface, swimming upward, holding on for the last few seconds and bursting into the air.

Arnold heard the motorboat behind him and turned to watch his brother drop a ski, then when the boat was past, he swam to shore. Sandra was sitting on the edge of the dock, her legs dangling. When he got to the dock, he reached out to seize her feet, as if to pull her into the water, but she lifted them away from him and walked back across the dock to sit in the white wicker chair. As he climbed out of the water, she was studying him, with a cool, distant look he couldn't understand, and then she bent and picked up her magazine and began to read. He turned away from her. The water in the narrows between their island and the one closest was still a little choppy from the passage of the motorboat a few minutes before. Waves spread from the boat and struck the shore, then bounced back from both sides to meet in the middle, in a complex pattern of tiny moving peaks. The ski that Donald had dropped tossed among the waves.

Arnold dived in and stroked easily out to where the ski floated and, pushing it ahead of him, kicked his way back. As he reached the edge, he saw Sandra on the dock above him.

"I'll take it," she said, indicating the ski. He lifted it toward her, and as she bent to catch hold, he saw the curve of her breast.

Sandra laid the ski on one side of the dock, and as Arnold climbed up, she stood beside it, unmoving, as if she were listening for something, perhaps the distant buzz of the motorboat. Or something else, farther off.

"What shall we have for supper?" she said, but as if that was not what she was thinking.

"Anything," Arnold said. "Sandwiches."

"We had sandwiches for lunch."

Her head was still turned a little away, listening. Arnold noticed a tiny bruise at the back of her thigh, and at first it seemed like a wonderful discovery, something secret and special. Then he thought that perhaps his father had made that bruise on her.

Arnold walked to the end of the dock, where the water was shallow, and sat there staring through the water at the rounded rocks with their traces of seaweed, dark green, slimy to the touch. A school of minnows hung there, tiny bodies, almost transparent, only the eyes and spines seeming solid, the rest a mere darkening of the clear water.

The sound of the motorboat was coming close again.

"What about macaroni and cheese?" Sandra said.

"Sure," Arnold said.

He put his foot, white and gigantic, into the water, and the school of minnows turned like a scarf in the wind and vanished. Arnold looked up to see the motorboat cutting through the channel, his father looking backward and waving to Donald to tell him to drop the rope. Donald leaned to his left and turned in toward the island, then, a few feet from shore, he dropped the rope, and as the ski began to sink, he slipped out of it and swam to the dock, pushing the ski in front of him. Arnold met him at the dock to take the ski. He dropped it beside the other one as his father turned the boat in a wide curve to avoid fouling the propeller on the ski rope, and brought the boat to the dock. Arnold caught the bow rope his father tossed to him. As his father drew in the ski rope, Arnold tied the boat to its cedar post with a turn and a couple of half hitches. His father always insisted that it be properly and neatly tied.

The man steadied the boat and stepped on the dock.

"You're a good water-skier, Donald," Sandra said.

"Yes," Arnold listened to his father say, "Donald's good on the skis. I've wondered if we might try to build a jump."

"I'd be scared to death," Sandra said, "to watch someone I knew go over a jump."

"What do you think, Donald?" the man said. "Would you like to try jumping?"

Donald shrugged. He was looking toward his brother, and Arnold thought he knew what was in his mind, that this dialogue sounded planned, unnatural, like something they might have heard on stage at the theatre in Port Carling.

"What about you, Arnold?" his father said. "Would you like to jump?"

"It would take a while," Arnold said, "to build a ramp."

Donald was moving away up the stairs. He was disgusted that Arnold had joined in the scene. Sandra was sitting in the wicker chair, looking toward her new husband, who was running his hand over the patch of grey hair on his chest.

"I thought I'd make macaroni and cheese for supper," Sandra said.

"That sounds good." He dived off the dock, and when he came to the surface began to swim across the channel in his stiff but effective breast-stroke. Arnold looked toward Sandra, who didn't meet his eyes. He was aware of the poise with which she held her long body. He couldn't help staring at her.

"I've got some letters to write," Arnold said, and set off up the path. He went along the front of the house and then crossed the little valley to the cabin where he and Donald slept.

When he walked into the cabin, Donald was standing naked, rubbing his hairless body with a towel.

Donald looked up at his brother as he came through the screen door.

"I'll bet she sucks him off," Donald said.

"No," Arnold said. "I don't think so. She wouldn't."

"Yes she would," Donald said. "She sucks him off every night. That's why we have to sleep over here, so we don't hear them."

"I'm glad we're sleeping over here."

"I don't see why we have to come up here at all."

"He's still our father."

"So?"

"So we have to visit."

"We don't have to visit her."

"She's his wife."

"I'm not coming up here again," Donald said. "I don't care what he says."

"It's not that bad."

"I'm never coming here again."

"It's OK."

"You like her, don't you?" Donald said.

"She's all right."

"I see you looking at her. You think she's pretty."

"She is."

"Mother's pretty too. But she wouldn't suck him off."

"Cut it out," Arnold said. He picked up a book and carried it to the door. He'd been planning to write a letter to his mother, but he couldn't do that now.

"I don't want to talk about this any more," he said.

He took the book outside and carried it to the rocky point that rose over the water beyond the cabin. As he sat down there, he saw his father and Sandra coming up the hill from the dock. His father reached out and took Sandra's hand to help her up a steep section. They disappeared inside the cottage, and Arnold couldn't stop himself from imagining Sandra pulling off the yellow bathing suit. He remembered the tiny curl of dark hair.

He opened the book. It was the *Collected Poems of Dylan Thomas*, the first one that had come to hand when he decided that he wanted to get out of the cabin, and now he found that he couldn't concentrate. He thought of what his father might be doing to Sandra's naked body in the cottage across the valley. He wanted to know, wanted not to know. In Toronto, more than once, he had gone to their house at night and stood nearby, looking at the lighted windows, watching the lights go out.

Sandra came out of the cottage in shorts and a white blouse, two wet bathing suits in her hand, and hung them on the string that ran from the kitchen window to a hook in a large birch tree. She looked across the little valley, and when she saw him, his eyes turned toward her, she waved.

Arnold pulled on a T-shirt that he'd left lying on the rail outside the cabin and went across to the big cottage. Sandra was in the kitchen, his father in the living-room with a book.

"Need any help?" Arnold said.

"You could grate this," she said, and passed him a piece of cheese and a metal grater. She tore off a piece of wax paper. "Grate it onto that."

He thought that she was pleased that he had come to help. It must be hard for her, trying to deal with the two of them, someone else's sons. She did her best.

"What are you reading?" she said, indicating the book he'd set down on the counter beside him.

"It's poetry," he said, "but I wasn't really reading it. Just staring at the page."

"I don't understand poetry."

"You just listen to it, like music," he said. "If I read it out loud to you, you'd understand it."

"You should do that. You should read it to me."

"Maybe I will, sometime."

He wondered if his father was listening. He read biographies, history. Arnold couldn't help wondering, as he watched the flakes of cheese peel off and fall, whether Sandra had any real interest in hearing him read her a poem. He hated the thought that she was handling him. It was one of the things he liked about his mother; she was so nervous, so easily upset, that she didn't have that dreadful, detached, "adult" quality.

Sandra was very capable, not all in pieces like his mother. He remembered wrestling with her on the dock. He finished grating the cheese.

"Thank you, Arnold," Sandra said. Her blue eyes were holding his.

"I'll go and get the canoe ready," he said. As he walked through the living-room, his father looked up but didn't speak.

When it was time for supper, Donald didn't appear, and Arnold was sent to fetch him; he came silent and sulking.

"Maybe you should take Donald over to the dance with you, Arnold," his father said in the middle of the meal. They had been sitting in awkward silence, all aware of the pressure of Donald's disapproval, but unable to conquer it.

"Do you want to go?" Arnold said.

"No. I'll be OK."

Silence fell. Arnold wondered whether his father had tried to get rid of Donald so that he and Sandra could be alone. Another few days, and Arnold and his brother would be gone, and the two of them could do as they pleased with each other. Perhaps they would swim naked in the middle of the night and make love on the dock.

After dinner, Arnold helped with the dishes while his father read and Donald went back into hiding in the cabin. It was comfortable moving around the kitchen with Sandra. They worked well together. Over the lake, the sun was dropping in a ball of fire, painting the water with brightness.

Arnold put the canoe in the water just as the sun vanished behind the horizon of evergreens. The pressure of the coming darkness, the cool air, the sound of the paddle were a gentle containment.

He paddled until, turning past one final island, he saw the lights of Barney's in front of him. Across the water, he could hear music as the band started to play. They sounded better at this distance than they did close up.

Arnold stopped paddling, and the canoe moved more slowly over the calm lake. Through the wide windows of the dance hall, he could see the movement of bodies under the orange lights. The dance hall was attached to a resort hotel above it—had been for years, since long before his father had bought land here. His parents had found the island and learned it was for sale while they were staying at the hotel on holiday. Had they danced together here? Was that why his father wouldn't bring Sandra to dance where he had held his other wife in his arms? Arnold couldn't imagine it, his mother dancing. It was too commonplace for her. She would see something vulgar in it. She was queenly, and queens did not dance. Arnold thought of the boys on that dance floor pressing themselves into the soft bodies of their partners, rubbing against their breasts.

He didn't want to go to the dance. He thrust his paddle into the water, and the canoe moved away. He steered the canoe toward the far end of the lake, using the lights of Barney's and the lights of occasional cottages along the shore to guide him.

His mother had never danced. He was sure of it.

Arnold had paddled for some distance when he heard thunder, and gusts of wind began to push the canoe around. Streaks of lightning jumped across the sky and were becoming more frequent, and the canoe was controlled as much by the wind as by his work with the paddle. There was thunder and lightning all around now, and the air smelled of rain. A bright flash of lightning revealed the wooded end of a large island not far off, and Arnold struggled to turn the canoe toward the shore. If he didn't get ashore quickly, he would be swamped, and even as good a swimmer as he was could be drowned in the middle of this darkness and storm. He came close to the end of the island just as the rain started. What he could see of the shore was all rocks. Arnold tried to brace the boat with his paddle while he climbed out, but he slipped on a rock and fell into the water, soaking his clothes and striking his shoulder painfully, but he found his footing and dragged the boat against the shore, lifted it out of the water and set it on the rocks, leaning awkwardly on one side against a huge boulder.

Just above him, momentarily illuminated by a huge flash of lightning that made everything around blue and brilliant, was a stand of big pine trees that offered some shelter from the heavy rain. He made his way up the hill and ran underneath them, huddling against a trunk in the middle. Some rain was coming through, but not a lot. Arnold was shivering.

The wet clothes were drawing all the heat from his body. He found a place to stand up and undressed himself, wringing out each of the garments and laying them on the ground on a dry spot under the trees. He stood there, naked, in the shelter of the trees, still shivering a little as the cool rainy wind struck his skin, and he rubbed his hands over his body to warm himself. He wondered if there was a cottage further up on the island, if a man and woman lay together, listened to the rain, touching. The man rose over her, penetrated the secret place. A flash of lightning revealed Arnold's naked body, the erection that thrust itself into the cold air. He stroked himself. Sandra fought back, playfully, but strongly, until he forced her down. The sperm leapt from him, and he sank down, naked and beaten, under the pine trees.

Gradually, as he squatted there, the lightning grew less frequent, and the rain began to let up. When it was over, he put on the damp clothes.

Within a few minutes the clouds had blown away, and a quarter moon cast enough light over the lake that it was easy for him to get the canoe back in the water.

His father's island was dark and silent when Arnold arrived back. He slid the canoe out of the water and left it on the dock, inverted, so that the last of the rain water would drain out, then walked up the path from the dock, placing his feet with care so as not to trip in the dark. As he passed by the front of the big cottage, he thought he could make out a figure standing there. The moon had vanished behind the trees, and at first, he couldn't be sure. The shape moved, spoke. It was his father, wearing only a pair of white shorts.

"I was afraid you might have got caught in the storm," his father said.

"I did, but I got ashore on one of the islands until it passed." They talked in low voices, just above a whisper.

"You've got a good head on your shoulders, Arnold," his father said. "I should have known better than to worry about you."

"I'm pretty wet," Arnold said. "I better get my clothes off."

"Good night," his father said, and went back in the cottage, where Sandra lay in bed waiting for him.

When Arnold got inside the cabin, he could hear Donald's slow breathing. He undressed, and as he was about to get into bed, he felt a piece of paper on top of the bunk. He took out the flashlight that he kept in the drawer beside his bed and flicked it on, to illuminate the paper without waking Donald.

Donald had left it for him. The dim circle of light revealed an obscene but realistic portrayal of Sandra and his father engaged in a sexual act, with Arnold watching them.

Sandra's house was in a neighbourhood built on a small peninsula, surrounded by trees and heavy undergrowth. The lawns were a deep green, and the gardens were full of brilliant blooms, roses, peonies, hydrangeas, pansies, sweet peas. As Arnold got out of the cab, he saw on his left a small, overgrown hillside, all weeds and raspberry canes. The house was built in a sheltered hollow below the side of the hill. There was a stone path leading to the door and a bed of roses in the centre of the front lawn.

Arnold walked up to the door and knocked. As he waited for Sandra to come, he looked across the lawn on the side opposite the hill. There was a cedar hedge, and on the far side of it, a large brick house, with wide picture windows. Stephanie and Bill's house.

There was no answer, and Arnold knocked again. Even after a third, louder knock, no one came to meet him. How many pills had Sandra taken? Might she still be asleep? Or lying dead in one of the bedrooms?

He went along the side of the house to see if there might be a window or back door open where he could look in, shout. She must be in an odd state of mind, confused, distracted.

At the back of the house was a lawn with a large evergreen at the end, and below that, he saw her, sitting on a rock at the edge of the tidal flats that waited, bare and expectant, for the water to return. Arnold walked across the grass toward the slender figure. She was wearing a white blouse and dark green slacks, and her hair, whether by nature or art, was still dark, and as he approached, she continued to stare across the tidal flats to the silver water of the strait beyond. A fishing trawler was moving across the surface of the water, its poles and antennae making it look tall, slender, insect. It vanished behind an island.

"Sandra," he said, when he came closer.

She turned.

"Arnold," she said. "I'm sorry. I didn't know it was time."

"I may be early."

He sat down on a small rock near the one she sat on. Even at high tide, he thought, these two rocks must rise above the water, tiny temporary islands. In front of Sandra was a tidal pool, perhaps six inches deep. She had a twig in her hand, and when she stirred it among the weeds, he saw something move.

"There are living things in the pool."

"Yes," she said. "All kinds of them."

"What are they?"

She pointed her twig at something that was like a round underwater flower, an aster or dahlia, with thick multiple petals of a deep purple; a soft sea-petalled mouth. When she touched it with her stick the mouth closed into a tight green ball.

"Aggregate anemone," she said. "Barnacles. I saw a tiny crab. He'll be under one of the little rocks." She stirred her twig among a bunch of weeds, and a small, spiny, ugly fish, mottled white and brown, darted away. "A tiny sculpin," she said.

"Full of life," Arnold said.

"'The unplumb'd, salt, estranging sea.' That's the title of one of your poems isn't it?"

"Yes. It's a quotation from Matthew Arnold."

"I'm not a great reader, but I was looking through your books yesterday and I saw it."

"Why were you looking through my books?"

"Looking for clues."

"But why there?"

"Why not? I couldn't think of any place else to look. I've gone through all the drawers."

"There's no news."

"No."

She stirred the water of the tidal pool, and the petals of the anemones waved, small creatures darted for shelter.

"I think he's dead," she said.

"He couldn't have just gone away?"

"Where? The police have looked, asked questions."

"Did he have money with him?"

"I don't know what he had in his wallet. I never asked. His credit cards haven't been used."

"What happened? You didn't give me any details on the phone."

"I'd driven into Victoria to do some shopping. When I came back he wasn't here."

Across the tidal flats, Arnold saw white gulls, black ravens, strutting over the damp mud like pieces in an anarchic game of chess, their raucous cries a jeering commentary on the game.

"Did you have any reason to expect it?"

Again she stirred the water in the pool by her feet.

"Let's go in the house," she said. "I'll make us some coffee."

She stood up to walk toward the house. Her feet, long and slender, showed white and veined through the gaps in the sandals she was wearing. The dark slacks matched the colour of the heavy grass. She moved lightly, the sixty or so years of her life carried with ease, her figure still slender, almost tall, her stride long, but the skin on her hands and feet had a veined pallor, as if age was coming on her gradually from the extremities. She held the back door open for him, and he made his way into the large, bright kitchen, a breakfast area on one side of it, with a wide window looking out to the water of the little bay where they had been sitting.

Just to the right was an alcove, with another smaller window, covered with white glass curtains, and below the window was a sink. Sandra was filling a kettle.

"You'll have coffee won't you?" she said.

"Yes."

"Good. It will give me something to do with my hands."

She plugged in the electric kettle, took out a coffee maker and filter, measured the brown coffee into the filter. Then suddenly, almost in the middle of a gesture, she stood absolutely still, her eyes closed, her breath slow and deliberate, her arms at her sides, unmoving. Arnold wondered if he should speak, but it seemed better to respect the distance between them. He watched her chest moving with breath. The kettle was making soft sounds as the water began to heat. Sandra opened her eyes, began to move about the kitchen, putting away the ground coffee, dropping the spoon she'd used into the dishwasher. Then she came and sat down by the small table.

"It's very hard sometimes," she said.

"I can imagine. Or perhaps I can't."

"You lost Marie."

"But there was no mystery. Just one huge fact."

"I'm sure he's dead."

"Do you think he did it on purpose?"

"Yes."

She went to the counter and stood by the kettle, though it wasn't yet boiling. She stared down at it as if her concentration was necessary to make the water boil.

"It's good of you to come out, Arnold."

"I don't know that I can help much now that I'm here."

"Did you resent it very much, when Ross left your mother?"

"You know I didn't. But Donald did."

"We haven't seen him for a long time."

The kettle was boiling, and Sandra picked it up and began to pour. Then suddenly she had dropped it, and there was hot water everywhere, and she pulled back with a scream. Arnold was on his feet beside her, and she was crying in his arms.

"Are you hurt?" he said. "Did it scald you?"

"No," she said. "I'm sorry. I'm so sorry, Arnold."

He led her back to the chair and sat her down, then went to the sink and found rags to clean up the spilled water.

"You don't need to do that," she said.

"I'll just wipe it up. You sit there. It won't take a minute."

Arnold was aware that his knee was cracking as he bent to soak up the water. He remembered the slight-ness of Sandra in his arms. It was a long time since he had been touched by a woman, held a woman's body against his own.

The water wiped up, he wrung out the rag, left it over the edge of the sink, Sandra watching him from her place at the table. He went and sat down by her, and for just a moment put his hand on top of the two of hers, which were tightly clasped on the table in front of her.

"Why are you sure he's dead?" he said.

"When Ross and I were first together," she said, "he used to tell me how unhappy he'd been with your mother. How cold she was, neurotic and self-obsessed. He made me feel I'd saved him from that."

She looked quickly toward him, as if he might interrupt, argue.

"Please don't mind me saying these things," she said. "Just let me go on."

"It's all right. Tell me."

"Two or three years ago, Ross started to mention your mother in conversation. I thought at first it was just a matter of sorting out the past, trying to maintain some contact with his own youth. But gradually he talked about her more and more, and it wasn't like what he'd told me before. It was all happy. It was all exciting. All the things he'd talked about, all those cold, neurotic things, were just a kind of sensitivity in her, the very things that made her special."

Her eyes were wet, her face swollen and hot.

"Ross was everything to me. I had no children because he thought he was too old, he didn't want them. So he was all I had. I existed because he saw me. But more and more, he talked about Lorraine, as if she'd been his real wife all along. I was just some girl he'd picked up, some temporary thing."

"He was old, Sandra. Things happen to the mind."

"I think he killed himself, or let himself die, because he thought he could find her. After all those years with me, he wanted to be where she was. And what do I have left? Tell me, Arnold, what do I have left? I was just an illusion."

"He wasn't himself."

"I think he was. He sounded like a man who'd come back to himself after a long delirium."

"No, Sandra. That couldn't be."

"Was he happy with Lorraine? Was I just some kind of madness that afflicted him?"

"They were my parents. How could I know? For me everything about them was inevitable. She was difficult, had to be treated gently."

"He told me that she never touched him, that he'd come home needing companionship, and she'd be in bed with an attack of nerves. That they had no sex life. I spent years trying to make up to him for those things, trying to be the warm, comforting person he needed. And then he started to talk about how she was a special person, how she saw things in the world that no one else could see. How could he be so cruel?"

"He wasn't himself. It was probably something physical, something in the brain."

"There was nothing wrong with his brain. I talked to people in Victoria, at the brokerage. He was more astute than ever."

"I always thought he was very happy with you."

Arnold wasn't sure that the words were true, or if true, decent. Didn't he owe his dead mother some loyalty? It was thought right, in the contemporary world, to allow only the claims of the living, but that left judgment rootless, floating. Even without any sentimental soft-headedness about an afterlife, the dead did exist, as part of the living, an aspect of what we are, and if we gave them no respect, our being became thinner, slighter. But the words were spoken. He had taken the way of easy kindness, and he had done it without hesitation.

"Do you want to see the will?"

"We can't be sure he's dead."

"I opened it, the copy that he kept here, because I thought it might tell me something. I was afraid of what he might have done. He seemed to be trying to erase me."

"What does it say?"

"Nothing startling. The bulk of the estate goes to you and me and Donald, with a nice bequest for Julia."

"He wasn't trying to erase you, Sandra. Some quirk of old age had got hold of him."

"I'm forcing you to say all these comforting things, Arnold, and it's not really your duty at all. I'm sorry."

"Is there anything we can do, about tracing him?"

"We could hire someone. If you want."

"I don't know."

"It seems . . . bizarre."

"Yes."

"But how much time do the police have to look for a retired stockbroker who disappeared while his wife was out shopping?"

"We should hire someone. It can do no harm."

The conversation evaporated into a tense silence. Sandra was picking at a hangnail.

"How is Julia?" she said.

"Well, I suppose. She drove me to the airport. I see her, and we talk, but I don't seem to know much about her life. She's working on some big project with puppets. 'Everywoman's History of the World' it's called. All in puppets."

"Can she support herself doing that?"

"She works in a bar, waiting on tables."

"Hard work."

Once again speech evaporated into air. Arnold

looked out the window across the lawn and the tidal flats. A gull lifted into the air with some small marine creature in its beak.

"She and Ross always hit it off when she came to visit."

"She told me."

"She looks a little like your mother, doesn't she?"

"A little."

"I thought that must be it."

"More than that, surely."

"Yes, of course, she's a clever girl, and Ross likes clever girls. But there was something more. I knew it must be Lorraine."

"You shouldn't let it become an obsession, the things he said about my mother."

"Why not? What else do I have to be obsessed with? Most people here are obsessed with their flower gardens. Or their tennis game. Or their investments. But then there are a lot of people who aren't obsessed with anything. Probably those people are obsessed with dying, really, but we all try not to notice that."

There was an edge to her voice, and Arnold was afraid that she might be approaching hysteria. He reached out and put his hand on top of hers, which were still picking at the hangnail.

"Do you want me to try to find some kind of investigator?"

"No, I'll do it. I need things to do."

She drew away from him and stood up. She wanted him to go.

"Thank you for coming, Arnold. I should have arranged to meet you at the ferry, but . . . I didn't."

"Do you mind if I go and talk to the police? I need things to do as well."

"Maybe you can stir them up."

"I'll try."

"How long are you staying?"

"I have an open ticket."

"Call me later, will you?" she said. "I think I need to lie down now. I'll pretend to sleep."

"I'll call."

"Do you want to phone a cab?"

"No. I'll walk a bit."

"Thank you for coming, Arnold. I needed to say those things. At least I thought I did. Maybe it helped."

Arnold stood at the back door.

"I'll call later," he said and went out. He went round the house to the road and began to walk back the way the cab had brought him. The whole area was built on a hill, and the houses were large and expensive, with wide lawns that were an intense green in the half-shade of the tall trees.

Arnold was walking quickly, as if he might outrun the thought of his father, the words that Sandra had spoken, the memories. At the bottom of a long slope, he came out of the trees and into a neighbourhood where the houses were less impressive, the lawns smaller. On his right, not far from the road, was a marina. Most of the craft moored were trawlers, but across the water, at a distance, he could see another marina with dozens of pleasure craft, the masts of the sailboats white needles against a background of dark green.

On a telephone post across the road sat a raven, its black feathers gleaming in the light. It was cawing quietly as Arnold walked past. Then suddenly there was a loud squawk close behind his head. He jerked his head round and saw the bird turning away, but a few steps later he heard wings and another raucous caw. The bird was attacking again, diving at him, then pulling away. He heard its harsh conversation from high above, and then again it dived. He ran to escape.

3

Donald was in his office at the back of the tattoo parlour when he heard the Rat walking around upstairs. It would take her only a couple of minutes to throw on some clothes and appear at his door. While he waited, impatient to see her, not wanting to be impatient to see her, he took out his file cards and began to work through them. He kept one card for each property. Once a year he'd start a new card, and transfer the old one to a holding file. For some of the properties, he had cards going back nearly twenty years.

He heard the Rat's footsteps coming down the stairs, and he waited with a card in his hand until he heard her knocking, went out through the tattoo parlour to the door.

It was a hot day, and the Rat was wearing tight silver shorts and a black tank top. Sandals on her feet.

He opened the door.

"How are you, Rat?"

"You want coffee?" she said.

In the morning, before she'd put on make-up, and with her hair pulled back in an elastic, her face was pale, and her eyes looked bald and scared. He could see little wrinkles in the skin beside them. The top teeth seemed to protrude further than usual under the pale lips.

"Coffee and a cruller," he said.

"So I'm going to the doughnut store?"

"The coffee's better."

"The Greek place has better food."

"I want a cruller."

The Rat held out her hand. The sharp little nipple moved against the thin fabric of the tank top, and he could see the blonde unshaven hair under her arm.

Donald took five dollars out of his pocket and gave it to her. She'd buy herself coffee and something to eat and keep the change. By now there was a tacit agreement about it. She did the fetching, and he didn't ask for the change. At first he'd made it a game, asking some days, not asking others. If he asked, she gave him the change, otherwise not. Then one day, when he asked, she simply said there wasn't any. Donald was amused at the brazen lie, and let it go at that. Now he never asked.

She slipped the bill into a pocket at the back of the shorts and turned away to walk down to the Danforth. Donald watched the pale legs moving away, and then closed the door. He'd have to be careful about the Rat or she would close those sharp little teeth on some tender part of him and hang on. He wouldn't have that, but he couldn't stop himself from liking her, her toughness, her brass, the smooth tightness of her little body, her carelessness.

Donald had anticipated trouble from the day she arrived to rent the apartment. As they stood in the empty rooms, she had told him her whole story, how she came from Peterborough, where she'd worked as a waitress, then in a store, and then as a cleaner with a maid service, how the last guy she'd been living with did nothing but drink, so that one day she'd taken everything from the apartment that was hers, sold it all and bought a bus ticket to Toronto. Her pale yellowish eyes were brightly focussed on him as she told him all this, wanting him to laugh or sympathize, demanding some response, and he found that he was listening, though usually when tenants started to tell him stories, he cut them off and got things back to business.

Donald lay back in the dentist chair in the middle of the tattoo parlour. Beside him was his work-table with three bottles of ink and a couple of needles. He hadn't cleaned them after he'd finished yesterday afternoon. Well, he had hours to clean them and drop them in the old dental sterilizer. He only did tattoos for three hours between four and seven. If that wasn't convenient, they could go somewhere else. Ed Wemp was supposed to be coming in today for an hour's work on the big crab on his back. When it was done, he planned to have the other aspects of his horoscope done on his shoulders.

The dentist chair was very comfortable. Donald often came out of his office to sit in it when he wanted to think something out. Rolf, who'd set up the business, had bought out a whole dentist's office to get the chair and the sterilizer and the tall white cupboard where he kept the needles and the ink. He'd gone to a lot of trouble setting up the store, with big blow ups of complicated tattoos on the wall, the dentist chair for working from the front, and a stool with a padded back for working from behind. But within a few months, he was spending everything he earned on white powder and getting behind in the rent. Donald was prepared to throw him out, but then he started to hang around and watch the tattooing, learning everything he could about it, and when Rolf was six months behind on the rent, Donald came in early one morning and found him with his teeth black and his head hanging and offered to take the equipment as compensation for the unpaid rent.

"What's my alternative?" Rolf said.

"To do the same thing the hard way. Lawyers, bailiffs, all that."

"Fuck it then," Rolf said and walked out. Donald never saw him again.

When he told Daphne he was taking over the tattoo parlour, she took it for a joke. He didn't reopen it for a while, not until he'd practised a bit, first on the skin of a half dozen picnic hams he got from a butcher store down the street, and then a couple of spots on his own shoulder, just to make sure. At first he'd only do simple tattoos, working exactly on the lines from a plate, but recently he'd become braver. He'd always been able to draw; using a needle wasn't that much different.

The Rat came through the front door with a brown paper bag in her hand. She put one coffee and a cruller on the table beside him and then went to the soft chair in the corner and sat down there with the rest of the contents of the bag, a black coffee and two double chocolate doughnuts. She curled her bare legs under her and sucked in a mouthful of the steaming coffee, then took a big bite of one of the doughnuts. Donald tilted the dentist chair forward and took his cup of coffee. It was hot and creamy and the coffee taste was strong and fresh.

"Why do doughnut stores have good coffee, Rat?"

"I don't know, Donald Duck. Tell me why."

"Must be that they sell a lot of it so it's always fresh."

"Maybe it's the doughnuts make it taste good."

She'd finished her first doughnut and was half-way through the second.

"You're hungry."

"I always eat a lot when I'm upset."

"Why are you upset?"

"Perry's driving me crazy."

"Is he screwing around?"

"If only."

"You're bored?"

"He can't get it up any more. It's driving us both nuts. He goes screaming off into the night and leaves me feeling like a dog with fleas."

"Tell him to leave."

"He says it's all my fault. It never happened with anyone else."

She lifted the cup of coffee to her lips and drank. Donald wondered what it was he liked so much about her teeth.

"You want to come upstairs with me?" she said.

"No."

"Why not? I never know when you will and when you won't."

"Not today."

Donald wanted to. She'd dropped her sandals on the floor and he couldn't help looking at her bare feet, the high arch and flat toes.

"When are you going to let me tattoo you?" he said.

"The day after never."

"I'd do something special for you. You've got good skin for it."

"Skin," she said, "good skin. Don't talk about my skin unless you're going to jump me."

"Not today."

She had finished the last of her coffee. She licked her lips.

"I think he's a fruit," she said.

"Perry?"

"I think he's a fruit. That's why he can't get it up."

"He used to manage, didn't he?"

"Maybe I wore him out." She gave a snort.

"Probably that's it, Rat. You'll spend your whole life wearing out one man after another."

"You think I should tell him to hit it?"

"I do."

Donald picked up his empty coffee cup and the wax paper from his doughnut, then went across and took the Rat's from the floor in front of her. He reached out and ran his finger down the smooth skin of her leg.

"You should let me tattoo you. It could be beautiful."

"I don't want to look like a freak."

"You wear make-up, don't you? It's the same thing."

"Make-up washes off."

"You just have to be careful to pick a design you like."

"Dragons or some shit like that."

"I've got a movie to show you," Donald said. "On the VCR."

"Where'd you get that VCR?"

"Bought it from a guy who came in for a tattoo."

"Is it hot?"

"Could be. It was pretty cheap."

"You should of bought me one."

"Are you a charity?"

"I'd have paid you off, you know, a bit at a time."

"I have enough trouble getting the rent from you."

"So what's this movie?"

"*Tattoo*."

"I might have known."

"I'll put it on."

"Not now. I've got to get ready for work."

The Rat worked as a cashier in a drug-store further east. She wore a yellow uniform.

"What time do you start?"

"Ten-thirty."

"How long does it take you to get ready?"

"Long enough. I've got to do my face."

She slid out of the chair and went to the door.

"See you later, Donald Duck," she said as she went out. He heard her feet on the stairs, then the sound of water in the pipes as she ran a bath. Donald locked the front door and sat back down in the dentist chair to plan out the day. He'd go and evict the old guy in the house on Major Street, and then he'd pick up a couple of subs and take lunch to Daphne at the store. He should clean the tattooing needles before he went. A dream came back to him, a dream he'd had last night. A trial for murder. They had pictures of someone being ripped up by tattooing needles, a body covered with cuts and blood, but it wasn't Donald who was on trial. He was there as some sort of expert witness, but once they got him on the stand, they started trying to prove that he had some connection with the murderer. It was a young man, someone related to him. Like a son.

Maybe it was Jeanie's kid. He hadn't heard from

her for years. For a while she'd write to him every now and then from that town in Ohio and ask him for money, and he always sent something, but for the last few years there had been complete silence. She'd never told him the kid's name, only that it was a boy. He'd be nearly eighteen now, almost grown up. Maybe someday he'd arrive at the door.

He'd never told Daphne about the boy. Couldn't. When they were trying so hard to have a baby, she'd done a lot of speculating about whose fault it was that she never got pregnant, whose body had let them down, and when she started agitating for him to go to a doctor, he'd been tempted to tell her. He didn't like medical men, and he wasn't going to have his semen put under a microscope, the little swimmers counted and denounced. Since they'd bought the dress store, Daphne worried less about it.

He put the needles into the container of fluid and plugged them in. Back in the office, he went through the last of the cards. Two or three people had called demanding repairs, and while he was sitting there, the phone rang, and the answering machine started. This office number was the only one he gave his tenants, and he left the machine on all the time. That way he could avoid confronting them except in his own good time.

In the other room, the tattoo needles were buzzing like two huge playful bees. He went and put some water in the sterilizer and plugged it in. It took a couple of hours to boil dry, and by then he'd be back. He checked in the drawer underneath and noticed that he was almost out of the antibiotic ointment that he used on the skin before and after tattooing. The Rat got a deal on it at her drug-store. Tomorrow morning he'd have to ask her to get him some.

What kind of design would he put on the Rat if he had his chance? He tried to remember what her zodiac sign was. Capricorn, he thought. A goat dancing down her back, one horn curving across each of the buttocks. She'd never agree to anything that big. Maybe just a little snake across the side of her hip where it would be covered by even a small bikini.

Donald spent too much time thinking about the Rat. Too much time observing her clothes, designing ornaments to paint on her skin. She was nothing to him; she was just the Rat who lived upstairs. He should stop thinking about her. He would remain, in every way that mattered, faithful to his wife. If he soiled a strange bedsheet now and then, it was a matter of no consequence. It was momentary and discreet and unimportant.

As he drove west along the Danforth, Donald considered his father's disappearance. Arnold had come back more convinced than ever that their father was dead, but there was still no proof. If the body didn't appear, they'd have to wait and go to court to claim their inheritance. There was a little shopping centre in Mississauga that some people wanted him to come in on, and a factory renovation down near Richmond Street, but he wouldn't have that money in time. He'd have to go to the bank. Just as well. He'd worked out some figures a few days before on the relationship of debt to equity on his properties and decided it was time to do some borrowing. When his equity started to get up toward fifty percent, he was getting too conservative.

On the Bloor Viaduct he looked north and south across the wide space of the Don Valley spanned by the bridge, and felt, as always, that he was driving through the air, and his breath caught until he reached solid land on the far side. He turned down Parliament, then west on Wellesley, around Queen's Park, then along Harbord and into the back lane behind the house. Two of the neighbours were busy renovating. It was probably one of them, locked into a renovation he couldn't afford, panicky about the investment, who'd phoned the building inspectors. A couple of months before, he'd got a series of work orders on the house, the main issue being the number of occupants. Donald had broken it up into individual rooms because he didn't feel like spending the money to make apartments. When he bought the house, he'd intended to turn it over quickly; the south Annex was a fashionable neighbourhood, a good short-term investment, and he'd got the house at a reasonable price because he had ready cash, but then prices had fallen, so he'd decided to hang on for a year or so. Renting rooms was simple and lucrative, but then someone had turned him in, and the work order had demanded that he add expensive new fire escapes and get a boarding-house licence.

Donald didn't like being bullied, and he'd decided to let the house sit empty. See how the neighbours liked the rats and derelicts who'd take it over. He didn't care if it fell down. The land was still worth a lot, and it would give him a warm satisfaction to drive by and see the house rotting, a decayed tooth in a mouth of perfect dental work.

The grass in the yard was tall and full of noxious weeds, dandelions and lamb's quarter and Queen Anne's lace. Let them grow strong and spread their seeds into all the neat gardens of the neighbourhood.

Donald went in the back door of the house. There was a smell of rotting food, and on the soiled green carpet lay a pair of men's underpants, red with white elastic. In one corner was a narrow mattress that someone had left behind, and taped to the wall a poster from a Dylan album. It was back in the days of Dylan and Janis Joplin and Jimi Hendrix and Joe Cocker that Donald had planted his seed in Jeanie's soft little belly. That was a long time ago. He couldn't believe that they weren't all dead, those singers. It was in a room not far from here that he and Jeanie had made love, late at night after he'd finished driving cab. He worked all day, in those days, selling flooring and carpets and supervising the installations, and then the second he got off work, he'd take over old George Lughanis's cab and drive until he was ready to drop. He had a key to Jeanie's room, and nights when he felt like it, he'd climb the three flights of stairs, and open the bottle of Scotch, put on a record and fall into her narrow bed.

As Donald went quietly up the stairs of the house, it brought back the feeling of all those nights. He'd just bought his first couple of properties, and sometimes, in the middle of the night, he'd wake in a panic worrying about meeting the mortgage payments, being able to get money ahead for the city taxes. When Jeanie told him she was pregnant, he'd gone a little crazy. He was too tired and too scared to handle anything else. They'd fought about it two or three times, and then she was gone. Back to her home in the States. Donald had been relieved. It gave him more hours free to work.

Those were high old times. It was just after Jeanie left that he found himself one night drinking in the Winchester, waiting to meet someone who never turned up, and a table away from him, out of place among the neighbourhood drunks, was a raggle-taggle bunch of young political activists who were

talking loudly about their battles against Meridian
and the other developers who were assembling land
for high-rise projects in the area. Something in the
sound of their words, some smoothness, some com-
placency, made Donald suddenly aware that they
were going to win some of these battles, and he knew
that if they did, the area between Parliament and the
river would be taken over by the middle class and
property values would go up fast. The next day he'd
bought a house on Sumach that he couldn't possibly
afford, and he'd gone even further toward the edge of
disaster within a couple of months by buying two
more. But within two years he'd taken his profit on
them and moved on. He'd had a soft spot in his heart
for John Sewell and company ever since.

Donald opened the door of the old man's room. For
a minute he thought he was dead. The pale face, with
its little grey moustache like something from a 1930s
movie, lay on the pillow, motionless, empty, the eyelids waxen and transparent. Donald looked carefully
and he saw the slight movement of breath. The room
was arranged in an orderly fashion, no clothes left
lying out, no fast food containers. On the wall over
the dresser was a nude clipped from *Penthouse*, firm
cheesy flesh, big breasts and fur the colour of a
groundhog's. A pair of grey, double-knit trousers
hung over a straight chair in the corner of the room.
On top of the cheap chest of drawers, one leg broken
off and resting on two halves of a broken brick, was a
plastic carrier bag with a bar of soap, shaving cream
and a safety razor. Beside sat a birthday card with a
picture of two mallard ducks flying across a gaudy
sunset. On the floor beside the bed stood a bottle of
rye and a tumbler.

Donald went to the chair and lifted up the trousers.

He reached in the pocket and pulled out a keychain with one key on it, the one to the front door of this house. He put it in his own pocket and returned the pants to the chair.

The old man must be seventy, and he only had one key. No car key, no key to the place where he worked, no keys to the houses of family and friends. What kind of a man had no keys? Donald hated failure. It made him angry. He went to the bed and shook the old man awake. The eyes stared up at him in terror, and as the old man spoke, his breath smelled stale, sour.

"What do you want?"

"I told you to get out. Find yourself another place."

"I'll pay you. I always paid my rent."

"I want you to get out."

The old man pulled himself up to a sitting position, gathered his little dignity. He was sleeping in a white T-shirt with paint marks on it.

"You said you'd try to find me another place."

"I looked. I've got nothing open."

"I can look after this place for you. Keep it clean."

"I don't want it kept clean. I want it full of rats and cockroaches."

The old man looked confused.

"I'd do a good job of it," he said. "I can keep a place clean."

"Just do a good job of getting out."

He reached in his pocket and took out the key to show to the man.

"I took your key."

"You had no right to do that."

"It's my house. It's my key. If you're not out in two days, I'll put your stuff on the street."

He turned and went out. The house was quiet

around him. It was no wonder the old man wanted to stay. He had the house to himself. He hadn't paid rent for two weeks since the others had left. You couldn't get a better deal than that, could you?

The encounter with the man in the bed had left him all on edge. He'd go down to Daphne's store and one of them would go out to the Korean place for something. He got in the car and drove it fast down the lane and out onto the street, slicing into traffic without stopping at the corner. He heard brakes squeal behind him, and moments later a cab drove by and he could see the driver's mouth moving behind the glass, shouting at him. Donald smiled and waved.

The longer he was in the property business, the more he hated failure. The old man could have worked harder, saved some money, bought himself some kind of a little house. Nobody needed to end up like that. Well, Donald had chosen the business, now he had to live it out. Supposed he'd chosen it, or been chosen by it. At seventeen, he'd reached the point of adolescent explosiveness when he couldn't sit at a school desk for one more day, so he'd walked out and started on his own. There were offers of help, but he wouldn't let his father run his life, slip him into some comfortable office where he could work his way up. To take anything from his father would have made him the old man's pimp, and he wouldn't be that. So he took whatever jobs were going, and invested in old houses because it was the only way you could put together a stake with little or no capital. Sometimes it cost him, but he'd learned the routine and now it was almost natural. He had equity, and he owed no favours, no debts of gratitude, except to Daphne.

Donald parked illegally in front of the store, and got out of the car. He wanted to see Daphne. He was all tied in knots. In the store window was a display of three flashy red dresses. *Big Girls* said the sign on the glass in front of them. It was a good idea, a store for fat women. She had a steady clientele who felt at home there, knew they weren't in danger of coming out of the dressing room and finding someone like the Rat standing there in her shorts and tank top. Daphne was still a good-looking woman, but she was big enough that the obese could feel comfortable with her.

Donald opened the front door, and his wife looked up from the cash desk.

"They were in from down the street," she said. "Somebody broke in again last night. Cops there, the whole thing."

"That kid on the top floor?"

"More of her criminal friends looking for drugs."

Donald turned and walked out of the store. As he climbed in the car, he saw one of the parking meter guys heading toward him. Donald was away before he arrived.

4

Perhaps he had never come back from the coast, was still floating among the islands, the delicate outlines, the glimmering water, the theatrical effects of light and cloud. He had imagined his father's body eaten by fish. He had driven along narrow roads where the rainforest grew tangled and close, where his father might have fallen, twenty feet from the road, and not been found for years.

Forest light. Water light.

His father had vanished, if Sandra was right, into his own past, into a secret story which he had kept hidden behind the proprieties of his life.

Arnold stared down at the familiar book. He had bought it for his mother, how many years ago. He was at university, and he had been looking, without success, and finally a little desperately, for a suitable Christmas present for his mother, when he discovered on a bookstore shelf a collection of translations from Chinese by Amy Lowell, years out of date, but somehow still there and for sale. His mother was not a great reader of poetry, but Arnold felt this collection might appeal to her. And she had liked it, had spent Christmas night reading it, her dark eyes concentrated and intense.

"That's a beautiful book," she said as she put it down. "You should read it."

When he did, over the holidays, by the fire as it stormed outside, it sank deeply into him. The simplicity of the lyricism stirred him. He was astonished to realize how many of these poems had been written more than a thousand years before. He was led onward to other books.

China became, remained, a central mystery. After Marie's death, friends had invited him to join them on a tour of the ancient Chinese cities, but he had refused, and as he received their postcards, he more and more felt that he had been right. This was the age of journalism. Everyone had to travel, to touch, to put their hands in the wound. The world was enslaved to actuality. But for him, China was an object of contemplation; what was desired and not attained became a focus for an inward intensity. Even Arthur Waley, he told his friends, the greatest English translator of Chinese literature, had refused to go there when he was offered the opportunity.

He looked around the conference room. Here they sat, the group of them, unrelated except by certain conventions of power and language and thought. Arnold did this, over and over, had for years, exchanging words, seizing the moment when it was possible to infect others with his own convictions, or abnegating when the problem became formless, when he could perceive no pattern in the feints and counterfeints of self-flattering ambitions. Arnold was skilful at the genial patter, the sudden shift of ground, the pretence of tenacity followed by apparent capitulation, the dogged repetition of simple things that would not be heard. Once he had wished to shine in such meetings, but now he preferred seeing things fall into place without apparent effort on his part. An Horatian concealment of the means.

"The minister," young Nigel Finch was saying, "thinks things can be done better."

It was an ugly face, Arnold thought, though the features were even enough, the nose straight, the reddish hair carefully cut, the carroty moustache fashionable in shape. The skin had the floury, transparent quality of a half-cooked crêpe, and the eyes were flat, glassy.

"Of course, Nigel," Arnold said. "Things can be done better. But they can, in a pinch, be done worse as well."

A tap on the conference room door, and Lydia Malcovitch, his secretary, excused herself and pushed into the room a trolley with coffee and juice. She had a genius for arriving just when Arnold needed a break.

"Thank you, Lydia," Arnold said. "I think we were ready for this."

She had two phone messages in her hand. She held them out to him, and Arnold glanced at the names.

"I'll get them later," he said. Lydia turned and left. It was only yesterday that she had come to Arnold in a quiet moment and told him about her investment in a Florida land scheme that more and more appeared to be fraudulent. The money was already paid and probably lost. He had put her in touch with a friend who was a member of the provincial police unit dealing with such schemes, and he was trying to reach a lawyer, an old connection of his father's, retired now, but an expert in the field of business frauds. If anyone could help her, these men could. If they couldn't he'd try others. As he listened to Lydia, Arnold had been unable to quite make out how the kind, sensible soul had been taken in, why she hadn't approached him for advice earlier. She had been afflicted, perhaps, with some glittering vision of herself as a worldly person, cleverly manipulating her savings into a stylish and comfortable castle for her old age.

He had brought her flowers this morning.

Arnold got himself a cup of coffee, black with sugar—his gesture toward lowering his intake of cholesterol, though the coffee was probably worse for him than the cream. He tried to avoid these magic actions, but now and then one took over a corner of his existence. A talisman against fear. He sipped his coffee and looked across at the window. Outside it was a grey day with a little light rain. At the far side of the table, Nigel Finch was crouched beside Patricia Van Zuylen, the young woman who was the academic expert on the committee, and she was turned sideways in her chair so that her breasts were close to the carroty moustache, the thick rusty hairs pointed vehemently toward their softness. Nigel had his arm across the back of her chair as he squatted there. He was attempting to charm the woman. Perhaps he was even succeeding.

Rain clicked on the glass. He must try to get away early and go to the museum. An hour of silence among the Chinese antiquities. Soon, perhaps, he would go back to New York to see the collection of

scrolls in the Metropolitan Museum. The scrolls at the
Metropolitan exhibited a wonderful range of calligra-
phic techniques, from the most cursive letters to the
most geometric. The landscapes too were rich and
varied. In one that had always delighted him, a painting of great rhythmic delicacy was created out of
short, thick, almost brutal brushstrokes. The trees
were simple letters in some abrupt alphabet, but each
one so tiny that when they were assembled in groups
of varying sizes and shapes, they gathered and dissi-
pated in swift waves of movement over the surface of
the silk.

To go back to New York. The last time, with Marie,
the cab through Harlem, going south on Broadway on
the trip back from the quietness—poised and fine, and
yet somehow specious—of the Cloisters. Marie was
ill; they both knew it but did not let on, not yet. Dark
men, black, Hispanic, filled the streets, groups gathered around benches, under a tree, near a store, as the
traffic poured by. Each block was its own village,
come together in the afternoon sun, adults and children gathered outdoors, escaping from the tiny, dim
apartments into the vivid life of the streets.

There was smoke in the air. Arnold watched out the
cab window and saw the dark smoke flowing from a
third-floor apartment. Flames danced in front of the
space of an open window. The windowsill was burning eagerly. Arnold could hear a child screaming. In
the delicatessen two floors below the burning apartment, the proprietor continued to serve customers.
Much of the crowd on the street ignored the event. Far
off, a sound of sirens.

The windowsill burned. What was inside? A rendering of hell, flowers of fire painted on the white
walls. A room filled with smoke and the screams of a

child. He thought it was his child. He didn't mention the screams to Marie. He couldn't. He hoped she did not hear them. Marie was ill. At the Cloisters, they had studied the tapestries in which the unicorn was murdered. The screams grew faint. Further down Broadway, the crowds knew nothing of the fire. They laughed. A black bus-driver, coming off shift, with a plastic cushion under his arm, waved his newspaper at two friends who stood talking at the curb.

"I wanted to thank you, Arnold."

Doris Camberly was standing close at his elbow and looking up at him. She had bright, youthful eyes, though she must be well over sixty.

"Why?"

"For getting me on this committee."

"You're here because we need you."

"And I need the money."

"It's not much."

"I know. An honorarium. A token. But when you're as broke as I am, it counts. Believe me, it counts."

"I didn't know things were that bad."

"Not bad. Just poor. A trip to Toronto, a room in a decent hotel, a few dollars to take home, it's a treat. I know I owe it to you."

"You deserve more than that, Doris, for the work you've done over the years."

"Stop being cool and polished, Arnold, and let me say thank you."

"All right."

"Thank you."

She put her hand on his arm and returned to her place at the end of the table. The warmth of her touch lingered. Nigel Finch was watching from his place on the other side of the room, had seen Doris touch his arm. Nigel turned back to the woman beside him and stared more intensely. Choosing sides. Winning converts. Did Patricia Van Zuylen find his pasty face attractive? Did she like the thought of the prickly red hairs of that moustache scratching against her skin? Perhaps it didn't matter how he looked. Don Juan need not be handsome to rouse desire, only determined and alert and intensely concentrated. Like prayer and mathematics, seduction called for a specialized kind of attentiveness. Perhaps: it was not his field of work.

The dreamer is occupied with the attempt to remember the name of the city. In the night streets he is surrounded by obscure threats, groups of figures that stare toward him and begin to close in, but he can't stop thinking that if only he could recall the city's name, all this would be settled. He knows that the water flowing everywhere should tell him something.

Even as he is beating off his assailants, his fists pounding futilely, then helplessly, he is sure that the name of the place would help him.

He has killed one of his assailants, and now he is running away, and each time he comes to one of the canals, he leaps across, but as he is in the air, the canal grows wider, and he falls in just before he reaches the far side. He is in the water, and a woman is pulling on his legs, to drag him downward. He can't tell whether she wants to be rescued, lifted from the water, or whether she wants to take him down and drown him. He is convinced that he can pull her up with him into the dim maze of the streets, but his strength is going. He is in mortal danger.

There is another woman in the water, beside him, stroking his face, as if in tenderness, unwilling or unable to see that he is being drowned. Perhaps she wishes to distract him, destroy him. He is kicking at the body that drags him down, in a desperate struggle to save his life. Vehemently, determinedly, his feet kick the face that is below him in the water, and just as he realizes it is Marie's dead blank face he is kicking, he finds himself somewhere else, alone in a silent square, the doors shut against him.

Arnold studied the pale green cover of the book in front of him. *The Kindly Institutions.* Patricia Van Zuylen had created it after an indefatigable survey of the various charitable bodies active in nineteenth-century Ontario. He imagined that pale round face hovering over desks and tables for untold hours of statistical reckoning. It was a worthy book, even, from time to time, an interesting one. It evoked a vision of the lives of the unfortunate of that time: the crippled road builder with his grotesque limp and missing hand; the Irish whore with hyperthyroid eyes bugging out of her head; the mad old woman sleeping in the streets, not yet captured for incarceration in the Queen Street asylum; the orphan boy who laboured as an indentured servant and grew sick sleeping in a shed; all these objects of care by the various Chari-table and Benevolent societies. The book made them real, but still, the thought of the drudgery involved in its creation stupefied him.

Lazy. He must be lazy, a useless parasite living on the public, while this small, neat young woman ex-hausted herself day after day over old ledgers, count-ing bodies, counting coins, assembling one of those immense statistical gatherings that they called history now. The discipline had undergone a revolutionary change in his lifetime, from the days when it was a study of political documents and heroic biographies, the battling-it-out of Whig and Tory traditions (with the mad visionaries like Spengler and Toynbee setting off their fireworks in the background), through the period of statistical accumulations, to the recent incursion from France of the study of *mentalités*—most usually the mentality of some obscure outsider, a renegade astrologer or homosexual dwarf.

He was outside it all. He had just come back from lunch with Julia. How fierce she was, his daughter, with her wild-coloured hair, the suddenness of her movements; like some startling woodland bird, visible, then lost in the trees. He had offered to give her money, an advance on what she had been left in his father's will, but she turned it down, bridling at the thought of indebtedness. Her eye was so clear, her resolution so firm. It was something he admired in her, even if it made her seem a little hard and inhuman.

Did Julia find him equally odd, incomprehensible? If nothing worse. Parents were so often the ghosts at their children's feast. Arnold was haunted; Marie's life had been scarred by her father's wounds. The man had gone to the Second World War when Marie was too young to remember him and returned one-legged, shell-shocked, a nervous wreck, a dangerously weak man who had to be catered to by his wife and daughter. He couldn't bear noise, crowds, disorder of any kind. Arnold had dragged Marie out of that house of death, into a steadier, sunnier life, and she had helped to dissipate the fouled intensities of his own youth into the decencies, the regularities, of their marriage. Their first apartment had been chosen for its light, because it faced south, and they had painted the walls white to catch and reflect each day's sun.

They had crawled from a jungle of familial complexity into this clearing. This white room. Where they could see the sky.

"Good morning."

Patricia Van Zuylen stood at the door of his office. She was prettily dressed in maroon trousers, a blouse with pale pink stripes and a corduroy jacket of a soft grey. She looked younger, happier. Arnold canvassed the discouraging possibility that it might be because of an affair with Nigel Finch. He hoped not. He wanted to think better of her than that.

"I hope you don't mind that I arranged to come in before the committee meeting."

"Not at all."

"After the last meeting, Nigel and I got talking about how much important archival material existed, scattered around the province, and how much was in danger of being lost."

"You must have converted him. I didn't think the material itself interested him much."

"He sees its importance now."

Arnold watched her eyes, to catch clues, to see whether the two of them were lovers, if this small fine body blossomed under the redness of that other—not that it mattered, only that he wished to know. To sit back and observe, to understand, to see the world grow transparent before him and reveal its mysteries, this was his role now. To see and suffer, like a wise old priest.

"What is it the two of you have in mind?" he asked. He would listen patiently.

Another white room. A room that might have been invented only for this, the Mediterranean sun patched in gold on the white walls, and the air stirred with wind off the sea. A solitude, surrounded by foreign faces, foreign tongues. A silence that was absolute as freedom might be, as dreadful. The light a slick shimmer on the pallor of skin. Marie's flesh like the flesh of a white rose, soft, and shivering with possibilities, history left behind; here anything is permitted. Intimacy, nakedness, freedom, delirious, appalling. Flesh white as the flesh of a rose, awkward, vulnerable and shamed, human.

Beyond the room, forever, was silence.

In front of him sat a wooden tray with the ceramic teapot he'd brought down on Spadina, and a flowered porcelain cup and saucer Lydia had given him for Christmas last year and which he used every day, though he didn't altogether like it. The fineness of the china was pleasing, but the pink flowers were not to his taste.

Bone china. What bones (whose bones) were calcined to make this delicate vessel? Held up to the sun, it would be almost transparent. Like the brittle skeletons of the old. Arnold drank the tea from his cup and set it aside.

On his desk was a small stack of blue message forms, calls that had come in while he was at a meeting at the Public Archives; he spread them across his desk and wondered which to answer first. It was an odd sort of work he did, wasn't it? Talking to people. Searching for agreement. Agreement on what? On the possibility of action in some arcane matters that had, in the long-term, some momentary or peripheral effect on the public good. Was the public good deeply affected by the manner in which the archives and museums of the province were organized? He was, currently, a minor priest in the cult of ancestor worship, provident in the name of the lost. The attempt to preserve the past, an objectified worship of the ancestors, had grown up as a central part of the modern, that dementia which took root in the Renaissance when both the past and the future assumed their excessive significance, their magic powers. History began, that absurd act of imagination that gave to time past and time yet to be a dangerous clothing of reality. To live, wide awake, in time, was the heroism of the modern world, but that heroism, like any other form, could be sentimentalized. And was, in most popular forms of historic endeavour. Most of the community museums were charming expressions of a local sentimentality about the past; the equivalent of family photographs, bronzed baby shoes.

Unfair? Perhaps. Perhaps, also, any act of remembrance deepened the note.

"Arnold."

He looked up, startled. Nigel Finch stood in the doorway, an unreal, almost distorted little smile holding his lips apart.

"Lydia said you might have a few minutes."

"Yes. Come in. Sit down. Talk."

"I don't want to interrupt."

"I was just reflecting on the relative unimportance, within the scheme of things, of what I do. The perfect moment to interrupt."

"I'd like your help, Arnold," Nigel said.

"How so?"

"I want to leave the committee."

"You don't need my help for that. Just quit."

"You know I can't do that."

"Why not?"

"What would that do to my reputation in the ministry? My first major responsibility, and I quit half-way through."

"Yes. It would seem odd."

"I need something that will make it all right for me to quit."

"A personality conflict."

"If necessary, but that's almost as bad. Can't learn to get along with others."

"Then why quit at all?"

"I have to. It's a personal matter."

"Personal meaning Patricia."

"Did you know? Does everyone know?" A hint of panic.

"I couldn't help noticing that the two of you were friendly."

"It was meant to be nothing more than that."

"Is there really anything wrong with the two of you being more than friendly? I'll keep you objective, never fear."

"It's my wife."

"Wife, Nigel, wife? I didn't know you were married."

"Well I am."

"I see. And your wife has guessed."

"Yes."

The face looked not just transparent now, but bald, skinless. Arnold felt a certain enjoyment in the young man's torment, but it was too easy to crush him now, to draw little drops of blood from his skin.

"You could just pull back. Stick to business."

"I told her that—Joan—but she doesn't see it."

"Joan is your wife."

"Yes."

"And you want to save the marriage."

"She's pregnant."

"Good God, Nigel. Why did you let her find out?"

"She guessed. She's very sensitive."

"And you're very insensitive, I suspect. Wanted her to know and forgive you, likely."

"I suppose you have no human weaknesses. Your wife has nothing to fear."

"She has nothing to fear, Nigel. She died two years ago."

"I'm sorry."

It was flat and abject.

"I'll find some way to get you off the committee, Nigel," Arnold said, "and without damaging your career. I don't know just how. I'll have to give it some thought. Perhaps something to do with enlarging the committee or creating subcommittees. I may demand someone more senior from your ministry. I'll tell you when I have something worked out."

"Thank you," Nigel said and stood up. Arnold watched him walk out of the room, and once past the door, turn a metaphysical corner into non-existence. Or as if he had fallen into the fabric of a book and was now at the bidding of Arnold's imagination. Imagine them, Nigel and Patricia, meeting one final time for a sweaty and sentimental parting, tied together at all the body's mouths, weeping and promising to re-member one another forever, and then tumbling out into the eternal night of non-being as Arnold forgot them. They went on, of course, existing for them-selves, somewhere, stubborn facts. In another five years, Nigel might cross his path.

Why did he picture so vividly their clandestine, adulterous couplings? Was it only his own sexual nullity? Standing as he did outside the eternal agoniz-ing arbitrations, the granting, exploiting, denying of power over the most inner secrets of the self, he was like a neutral country observing a war, awed by the huge, half-random acts of wreckage, the desperate, stupid heroism of the combatants.

Arnold had departed early from the field—fleeing from what he had learned, too young, of this carnage—into the decency of his marriage. One built a marriage, like a house, to function and serve the needs of the living. One dressed in it, as in suitable clothing. One kept safe from the dreadful nakedness that was passionate desire, the torture of grasping intimacy.

5

Unfair. It was, for after all she lacked nothing that she could quite put words to, but perhaps that was only because of her lack of skill, and if she had been, like Arnold, a person with authority over words, then, perhaps she would have been able to define the thing. The feeling was, by now, so familiar, so well-known to her, almost like a regular malaise associated with the time of the month. Once, even, when she had tried to hint to her friend Cathy what she felt, it had been taken for that, a mood, one of those female things, but it was not, was something subtler, more wide-ranging, more pervasive, and it did not come with the regularity of her monthly periods. Yet when it came, the recognition was immediate, and she knew that this one particular feeling had been with her all the time, alongside, or underneath all the others, and that she, a happy person she would have said, fond of her home, her husband, her daughter, her poised and decent life, was also someone lost and miserable, shut off from everything that mattered to her, even though she didn't know what those things were or might be.

She thought of it, sometimes, as a place. There was a phrase—the land of heart's desire—and she would try to picture this land, and never quite could, except that now and then, not often, she would turn a corner of the city, and the light would be shining, sunlight, just so, on a tree, or the porch of a house, and she would feel, momentarily, that she had caught a glimpse of what that place might be like, of how the way the light fell there would release something within her, and the knot of misery that underlay her happiness would dissipate and a new kind of stillness and serenity would pass through her, and she would love, fully, the things that now she loved so imperfectly. No longer would she bend to kiss Julia good night and feel between them some thin transparent wall, like a clear plastic. She would know, in the immediacy of touch, that this child was her own flesh. She would not be struck down by separateness and mystery.

Marie opened the drawer to choose her clothes— bra, panty-girdle, slip, stockings, all clean, all quite new. She would feel well-turned out, at least that, and in the tweed skirt, a sort of heather-colour, which she had recently bought from Holt's, and in the sweater of ivory cashmere, and with her hair carefully brushed, she would look, perhaps, not beautiful but almost elegant, well cared for, tasteful.

She had the day to herself. Julia was with Leanna, the careful, motherly Jamaican woman who cared for her two days a week. Arnold had insisted on that, that Marie must have some time free, that she have time to herself, and from the time Julia was six months old,

Leanna had cared for her two days a week. Marie had developed the habit of spending one of those days in the apartment, sewing, writing letters, putting Julia's toys and clothes in order, checking through Arnold's closet to see if any of his suits needed to be sent to the cleaners. Things like that, small necessary things. The other free day, she would go out. Those days were the hardest, for every week she was forced to confess that with a day to herself, she had nothing pressing to do. Now and then to shop, or pretend to shop, walking through stores, idly examining a dress or coat. Once a month or so, she would meet Cathy for lunch at some new restaurant, Hungarian or Chinese.

A day to herself. Herself. Who was that? No one much. Still, it helped if she dressed carefully, laying out the clothes on the bed and taking them up, one item at a time to put on, not looking in the mirror until the whole outfit was assembled, the slip pulled down, the sweater set straight at the shoulders, her hair brushed into place—though it would need adjustment once she had looked in the mirror. She would open the closet door, and look at herself, turning her head quickly from the right and trying to catch a momentary glimpse of herself as if she might be seeing a stranger pass by just at the fringe of vision. The woman she met in the mirror was not lovely, not striking in any particular way, but she seemed to be on top of things, in control.

Again she looked away from the mirror, turned her whole body to one side, and then glanced suddenly back to catch a quick look at this passing stranger in a tweed skirt of a grey-mauve, and a sweater of a soft colour just off white. The body was a little heavy, with a high thick waist. Nice feet, long and shapely. A pleasant, friendly expression on the face.

She took up a brush and standing by the mirror put her hair in order. It was rather fine hair, and she took some pride in its fineness, but it was not easily kept in place; still she hesitated to coat it with hair spray. She had seen too many women going about with lacquered hair. There would be no chemical shine about her, and no heavy coating of make-up on her skin. Just a touch here and there, on cheeks and lips and eyes to shape the face a little.

Marie tidied the make-up table, crossed the room and opened the glass door that led to the apartment balcony. Below, the trees had just come into leaf, and there was a canopy of pale green over the streets. A beautiful calm gentle colour. Underneath that canopy they walked and dreamed, the men and women, and the pale green light fell on their skin and made them luminous and kind. She could go down there and walk among them and meet one and smile and something in her would unfold like the leaves.

Unfair. She knew it was unfair, for Arnold was kind to her, and generous, and he was a respected man who was achieving positions of greater responsibility yet still made time for her and for Julia, but in spite of herself, Marie couldn't help thinking that somewhere, perhaps on the sunny spring streets, was the man, the man who would go with her through lanes and parks and gardens, in silence, knowing that they saw the same lovely momentary things, an old woman walking a dog, one of the first crocuses, a set of silver in the window of an antique dealer, heavy and old fashioned and yet right and proper and unmodern. Or more than that, she would see new things that before she might have missed.

Beloved. Dearest one. My love. She had never in her life used such words. Never. She might die with-

out ever once saying, oh my beloved, my dearest one,
my love.

It was unfair. It was wrong, that she could not stop,
on a day like this, the feeling that she was waiting,
that just around the next corner, somewhere in the
city, a man was waiting to whom she might say these
things. My beloved, my dearest one, my love. The
words brought with them the feeling of a room, fire
and deep shadow, a place far away from the world
and yet worldly, as complicated as history. A house
with long stairways and long corridors. Secrecy, that
was the centre of it. The words spoken were enriched
by the dark secrecy of the place where they were said.

Silliness, adolescent silliness. She stripped away the
romantic details and the whole dream died, and when
she repeated the words in her mind, my beloved, my
dearest one, my love, they had almost lost their power,
as if the one to whom they might be addressed, the
one who, in silence, would know her, would understand without speech, so that something in her would
blossom, was now dead and lost. Gone forever.

She stood high up in the air over the city. This was
Arnold's place away from the world, and in the
summer he would sit on the balcony in a fine Shera-
ton armchair which they had bought just after they
were married, and he would hold his notebook on his
lap and sometimes write a few words in it. The poems
came slowly now, or never, and Marie felt that the
failing was in her. She did not inspire him. She could
not. On the balcony, the noises of the city distant and
petty, he looked into the sky for poems, but none
came.

Marie had sometimes thought that they should
leave the apartment, invest in a house, but Arnold
was persuaded that buying a house was a trap. His

spare time would be taken up with the responsibilities that came with owning property. They would see all their money going into a mortgage and constant repairs. They wouldn't be free to travel. She accepted that he was right.

Small figures moved along Avenue Road. Men and women living their lives. From here, mysterious and special. If she observed them from closer up, they often seemed to her crude and obvious and vulgar. Perhaps Arnold had been right to bring her here to his safe place in the air. And if so, was it only some terrible feebleness in her that she did not turn to him in the night and say what now she could not say? No other man would be more considerate. He was a dignified man who could win the respect of others. He was, with his tall figure and straight pale hair and oval, well-featured face, handsome. In restaurants, she saw other women notice him. When she saw that, why could she not feel proud and take his arm and smile?

What was the knot that she could never untie, in Arnold, or deep within herself? What was it she longed for and could never name?

Marie closed the balcony door, took her suede jacket from the closet and left the apartment. Outside, she turned down Avenue Road and walked toward Bloor. The men and women she passed were beautiful and happy. It was good to be here in Toronto on this remarkable spring day, and she would have a fine time and then return home to greet her daughter.

Watching those who passed by or window shopping, she made her way along Bloor. She thought of getting on the subway and going up to Eglinton to explore a new district. She'd heard there were nice clothing shops there, on the edge of Forest Hill, but instead she crossed Bloor and travelled south, going into one or two stores, her fingers caressing the fabric of a blouse in one store, a jacket in another. She had no intention of buying anything, but the racks of clothes gave her a sense of eager possibilities.

A few blocks away a familiar restaurant had opened a sidewalk café. On the weekend she'd seen it from the car window. She'd go there for lunch. It was still too early, and she dawdled along the spring streets noticing how warm it was in the sun and then how suddenly cold when she crossed to the shaded side of a small street. As she went along, she found she was in an odd mood. Little details would spring to her attention and demand that she see and remember—a stain on the black tile below a store window, a pattern of scrap paper at the edge of the street, the face, still, round, dark eyed, almost oriental, of a little girl, who turned away from her mother who was studying a display of dresses, the careful eyes gazing at Marie. They were noticing each other with the same unexplained intensity, Marie and the child. She was about Julia's age, and Marie knew suddenly that Julia should be here with her, not abandoned to a substitute mother. Leanna was wonderful, of course. Marie wondered if she was too wonderful, too much warmer and more immediate than Marie herself. But she was black, Jamaican, African by heredity. Marie could not be like that. She remembered how, when they went on holiday to Jamaica, one of the black beach boys had stared at her in her bathing suit, bold, insolent, defiant, perhaps disdainful of her awkward body. She had run down the beach and thrown herself into the gaily coloured water and swam away from him. She swam well; he could not despise her for that. She had always wondered, never understood, what it was he saw when he stared at her. No one else had ever looked at her so boldly. From that day on, she had been uncomfortably aware of the gleaming black skin of the beach boys as they skilfully handled chairs and umbrellas and paddle boats. Her awareness had become a permanent and painful state, and she began to want to leave, could not enjoy the sun and the white sand and the blue water of the Caribbean, though she tried to for the sake of Arnold who had planned the holiday for her. Sometimes she saw Leanna looking at her and she remembered that black man, his reddened eyes, missing front teeth, as if Leanna might be the same person, but carefully disguised to win her confidence. She thought this, though she knew it was wrong and bad; Leanna was kind and warm and wonderful. There was nothing secret and reprehensible in her gaze.

The little girl was watching her intently, as if Marie might be someone she knew and feared. It seemed to Marie that the face she was staring at had the same expression as her own. She turned and walked away, and deliberately crossed a street into the sunlight, to wipe from her body a chill of consciousness which was too much like the chill of waking on a bad morning with a voice far at the back of her mind calling out a name over and over, a name that she could never quite hear, and she would curl her body into a tight ball and plan the events of the day, imagine waking Julia and dressing her and feeding her, planning until she had filled her mind with all the good things of her life and was ready to begin living.

When she arrived at the restaurant, one of the waiters, one she recognized, a tall Hungarian boy, was preparing the outside tables, spreading a tablecloth on each, placing a vase with a single daffodil. She chose one not too far out on the sidewalk, but with a view of the street.

"Please," the young man said, "sit down. I will come in two minutes."

He had a deep voice and a pleasant, half-cynical smile that made you feel that the two of you were enjoying a joke against the rest of the world. He was Marie's favourite waiter here. Once, when she had come with Arnold, the young man had told them a little about how he had left Hungary in 1956, little more than a boy, but determined to escape to the west.

Marie settled herself in a chair, her purse over the back, her hands on the table in the sunlight, close to the single pale yellow daffodil. She watched a woman pass by on the street in front of her, with a bag of groceries, one child held by the hand, the other propelled ahead of her, her face set in an expression of anger.

How spoiled Marie was, to be able to sit here, at leisure, to watch the world go by, to have the money in her purse to pay for lunch. Arnold was so thoughtful toward her, so loving.

The waiter was setting a table a few feet away. He had long legs, his dark trousers were tight. He knew that he was young and attractive, and he enjoyed it. His enjoyment allowed Marie to enjoy it as well. She would look at him, as she looked at the fresh, pale tissue of the daffodil. A beautiful thing offered to her by the world for her pleasure.

She ordered an omelette, and afterwards, espresso coffee and a pastry from a tray just inside the restaurant window, and she ate slowly and with pleasure, sunlight falling on the pavement at her feet, the movements of the waiter economical, graceful, as he served her. This corner of the world was her own, was special to her and the spring, and she would keep the rest of the city away. The street she watched was only a show for her enjoyment.

Minutes later, the city invaded, as the city would always do. She saw a familiar vehicle, a half-ton truck, and recognized the driver as her husband's brother, Donald.

The last time she had seen him was in the winter, the week-end when she had gone with Arnold to meet his brother at their mother's house and begin disposing of her possessions.

A cloudy Saturday morning: there was a little fresh snow from the night before on the circuitous Rosedale streets, and as they pulled into the driveway, they saw Donald's half-ton truck in front of them, and a single line of footsteps across the snow to the back door of the large brick house. The snow on the front walk had not been shovelled for the past three weeks and the property had an abandoned look, made grimmer by the dark sky. More snow would soon fall.

Marie and Arnold got out of the car, and crossed to the back door, the new snow slippery on the frozen crust of the old, that crust sometimes breaking under the weight of their bodies. Inside the back porch was a pile of clay plant pots, mostly empty, one or two with dried stems sticking out of the hard earth. The kitchen was clean and bare. Mrs Armitage, the cleaning woman who appeared once a week by cab at the front door, and then vanished at the end of the day somewhere into the little streets of the east end, had come in after the funeral. There were no lights on in the room and in the bleak winter daylight, it was sad and haunted. As Marie bent to take off her overshoes, Arnold pressed the switch and the bright lights hurt her eyes. Arnold slipped off his rubbers, and they went through into the hall, still in their coats, though the house was hot and close.

"Donald?"

"I'm up here."

Footsteps, and he looked down at them from the top of the stairs.

His face was pale, his dark eyes focussed with the intensity of hatred, the lips were oddly shaped, as if to receive a harsh demonic kiss. Marie was afraid that within a few minutes of starting the removal of his mother's traces from the world, Arnold's face would look like that too. She should have stayed home, left the two men alone with the woman who had haunted and dominated their lives. Marie had always been frightened of her, from the first time she met her, at the high school graduation, frightened of the intent eyes, the way she gripped Marie's hand when they were introduced, the fineness of the skin with its tiny wrinkles, the surprisingly deep voice, and behind all these things, a kind of nervous high-pitched buzzing, a sound that might be made by a bomb about to explode. Marie knew from Arnold, even then, that the woman was something of an invalid, always on the edge of nervous collapse, and it had amazed everyone that she had not gone under when her husband left her. She had taken to her bed, refusing to eat or see daylight, wandering through the house at night, tearful and lost, but she had survived.

Marie had not liked her, for she knew the woman regarded her as bland and pedestrian because she lacked the selfishness, the nervous self-indulgence that had made Lorraine Riggs's eyes glitter, but when she married Arnold, Marie knew that the mother came as part of the arrangement. They could not move away from Toronto. One of the boys must always be in the city, ready for her call. After all the years she hardly needed to pick up the phone. She only needed to feel a desire for their support, and one of them would arrive, play cards with her half the night, talk till dawn, drive her to the office of one of her doctors.

Looking up the stairs at Donald's darkened, angry face, Marie shuddered at the sudden realization that she knew those dark eyes, those twisted lips. Donald's face had become the face of his mother.

"Take off your coats," he said. "It's going to be a while."

Marie began to unfasten the buttons on her coat, but she knew she couldn't go near Donald, not as he was now. She could not go up those stairs and see the bed where the mother slept, where she'd been found dead, see the clothing that she had left behind. Orphan lingerie, deserted dresses.

"I'll go to the kitchen," she said, "and sort the dishes."

"That's a good idea," Arnold said.

Marie hung up her coat and turned away, without looking at her husband's face, lest she see that it too had taken on the features of the dead woman. Once in the kitchen, she opened cupboard doors, at random, looked at all the dishes and pots and pans and couldn't think what to do with them. The Limoges was in the walnut sideboard in the dining-room. The dishes and china in these cupboards were merely functional, to be sold or given away, she assumed.

In the back seat of the car were cardboard boxes. Marie pulled on her overshoes, and without bothering with a coat, she went out to collect them. The discomfort was a relief, walking with her overshoes unfastened, almost slipping, the crust of snow collapsing, the cold making her pull up her shoulders. Something simple, brutal, satisfying about the way the empty cartons knocked against each other.

When the cartons were filled, most of the shelves bare, except for one shelf with odd bits of silver and antique china that might be wanted, she walked down the hall toward the stairway. Upstairs they were arguing, and the vehemence of Donald's voice made her afraid for her husband. They were brothers and she should not intrude: Arnold was her husband and deserved any poor help she could give him. How to arbitrate the contradiction of those two statements.

She went up the stairs. The two men stood in the bedroom, a pile of cardigans on the bare mattress, half-filled boxes of slips, nightdresses, on the floor. Donald had a pile of notebooks in both his hands, gripped as if he thought Arnold might be about to snatch them away. Arnold's face was very pale and still, his mouth thin and cruel.

"We're going to burn them," Donald said. He turned his eyes to Marie as if he thought she would support him. He was so sure he was right that even Marie could understand.

"We don't know what's in them."

"We're not going to know," Donald said.

Arnold turned to her.

"Mother's diaries," he said.

"I'm taking them to the fireplace and burning them," Donald said.

"Why?" Marie said.

"They're hers. They're private."

"Maybe she meant them to be read, someday," Arnold said. "Nobody keeps a journal without the thought that someone may read it."

"Nobody's reading these."

"I think we have a right to look at them."

"No. You have no right. What she went through was her business. If she wanted us to know things, she told us."

"Then why did she write things down?"

"I don't know."

"I don't see any harm in one of us reading them. We're her sons. They belong to us."

"They're hers. She doesn't belong to us. Why do you want to read about what she went through? It's perverted. You want to hear how much she suffered? You want to read why she killed herself?"

"We don't know that."

"You got that doctor to say it was probably her heart. Your government friends talked to the coroner and kept it all quiet. But we know fucking well that she took too many pills."

Marie had been told none of this. Arnold had gone to the house, found his mother dead, made all the arrangements. He had been cold, silent, untouchable for days, but he had never spoken of suicide. Marie had to get out of the room now. They told her nothing. She was no part of the family. She had no place here. It was as if one tried to referee a drunken, unseemly brawl. When Arnold looked toward her, his grey eyes narrowed a little with an expression she could not read, she looked away.

"All right, Donald," he said, "you can burn them if you choose."

She could not interpret the tone of his voice, the expression in his grey, flat eyes. He was half-smiling, almost as if he might have won an argument but was restraining his triumph. It was all she could do to turn and walk away.

After that the day was merely laborious and distasteful. Marie was offered a lovely mink coat that her mother-in-law had owned, but she could not accept it, though she knew that her rejection hurt Arnold, made him dreadfully angry.

"You'll understand, Arnold. Later."

"Yes," he said. "I probably will."

They went from room to room, sorting, packing, burning. It was too much to attempt in one day, but Donald was determined to finish. He wanted to keep nothing, to give nothing away, simply to destroy everything, as if to wipe his mother's existence from the face of time. Had he been able, Marie was sure, he would have brought in wreckers and had the house torn down, every brick carted away, the ground levelled. In the fireplace lay a pile of leafy ash where he had burned his mother's diaries, pouring lighter fluid on them to speed the destruction.

They worked without stopping to eat. Donald brought in a thermos of coffee from his truck, and the three of them drank it, lukewarm and bitter. In the face of Donald's rage to destroy, Marie felt that she could save nothing, keep nothing from the house, but Arnold insisted on a few things, the good silver, the Limoges, and offered to pay Donald half their worth out of his share of the estate. Donald would hear nothing of payment, but he wanted them gone. They packed them and carried them quickly out of his sight. On the way to the car, Marie wished she could speak about Donald, the state he was in, but there was nothing she could say that Arnold did not know. He had, now and then during the day, made small attempts to calm his brother, but seeing that they would do no good, he had abandoned them.

They put their booty in the car trunk and returned

once more to the house. Through a window, Marie saw a bare bulb hanging in one of the upstairs rooms, stripped of its shade. The whole house was like that, stripped of its dignity, its humanity. Naked and help-less, unfriended. Marie was full of sorrow for the house, this passive victim.

Late in the afternoon, the winter evening growing dim outside, the last light pearly and sea-blue and pale green in the west, among clouds, Arnold called a halt.

"Another hour," Donald said, "and we can finish it. I have to drive cab starting at seven."

"You can work on alone if you like," Arnold said. "We have to rest and eat and pick up Julia from the baby-sitter. We have to go now."

"Go. Do whatever you like."

"We'll come back tomorrow."

"If you want. When I walk out tonight, I'm never coming back."

Donald began throwing beautiful linen napkins into a garbage can. Arnold watched him, then turned away, looked around the empty dining-room, slowly drawing in a breath through his nose as if he might be seeking out some suspicious odour. Then he glanced at Marie.

They picked up their boots at the back door. It was on the way across the snow to the car that Arnold slipped and fell, his feet shooting forward and his body going down rigid on the snow. Marie stopped and turned, expecting him to scramble up, half-hurt, half-embarrassed, but he lay still, as if dead or para-lyzed.

"Arnold?" she said, and moved toward him. "Are you all right?"

"Just get in the car," he said quietly, not moving.

"I'll be there in a minute."

She wanted to bend and touch him, to find out what the trouble was, but the quiet voice was distant, peremptory. She went and sat in the car, and Arnold lay on the snow until at last he got up, and came to join her.

"I could see the stars," he said. "Lying there, I could see the stars, and I didn't want to move until I remembered how many light years it is to Arcturus."

Marie sat at the restaurant table and brought a cup of espresso to her lips. She imagined Donald's rapid, half-distracted progress through the city streets, in his truck, or at night in a taxi, always restless, always moving. Where did he go when he could finally run no further? Did he fall into some narrow bed, dead-tired, alone? She knew Arnold worried about him. Arnold was a kind, concerned man.

She sat still, in the heart of the city, while Donald raced through its streets like a virus in the blood.

A woman came from the street and walked to a table, a few feet away from where Marie sat. She wore a pale mauve dress, the skirt cut quite short, and a white jacket that emphasized her dark eyes and eyebrows, thick dark hair. As she sat, Marie imagined her, that morning, looking into her mirror just at the same moment as Marie had looked in hers. She was an attractive woman, and when she looked in her mirror, she would see a supple, athletic body, bright eyes. Was she satisfied with what she saw? Did it make her proud and content? Or did she want something more, even while she realized her longing was impossible, unfair?

The waiter, the same one who had waited on Marie, now went to her table, and they joked, talking quietly with the intimacy of old friends. Or lovers? There was something flirtatious about the way they looked at each other. Perhaps this moment, as Marie watched, the woman was planning that later on she would meet the tall, smiling, cynical boy, and they would lie together, and this woman would say to him—as Marie had never said to anyone—my beloved, my dearest one, my love.

6

Donald was driving down a one-way street, the wrong way. It saved several blocks of circuitous turns. He saw a woman on a veranda waving at him, gesticulating, demanding that he go back. As he passed her house, she ran down the steps as if she might pursue him. Once past, he could see, in the rear-view mirror, the woman standing on the sidewalk, her arms in the air in a melodramatic gesture of desperation. She was wearing shorts and had thick legs that made her look dwarfish.

Daphne had good legs; trim ankles and long feet, but then above the knee they spread into wide, soft thighs. That morning he'd lain in bed and watched her as she came back from the shower. She knew he was observing her, and deliberately dropped the towel to wander around the bedroom naked as she assembled her clothes and started to dress. Her skin was as smooth and white as cream, and everything about her was round and lovely, heavy breasts with a huge circle of pink around the nipple suspended above the curving belly.

He was meeting her in a few minutes to go out looking for a new Doulton figurine. When Daphne was growing up, she'd known a neighbour, a doctor's wife, with a few Royal Doulton figurines, and in the early days, she'd told him how Doulton had become her idea of the ultimate luxury.

Donald had bought her the first one, an old lady with balloons, as a present, back when they were first married and there wasn't much money. In fact he'd got it cheap from a woman who'd boosted it from a gift store, but he hadn't ever told Daphne that. The day he'd given her that figurine was one of the few times he'd ever seen her cry. It made him sad, knowing it was stolen and he'd bought it at a bargain, but there was nothing he could do. As they got ahead in the world, they established the practice of buying a new figurine every time he bought a new piece of property. Donald had got a special glass-fronted case made for them by a carpenter who did some work on his houses. The man had been pleased to get a break from framing walls and had done a nice job, and now it stood in the living-room at the end of the sofa. Donald had fitted it with a good lock and an alarm.

There was no place legal to park near the store so Donald pulled up in his usual spot right in front.

Inside the door, he saw Joan, Daphne's assistant, behind the counter. Joan was a tall, broad woman with a mouth like a prize peony and hair bleached to a colour that was closer to gold than anything else.

"Daphne's out the back," she said, "with a sales-man."

"We're going out," Donald said.

"Probably she won't be long."

"Who is it?"

"The guy from Exclusive Dress."

Sheldon Zemans. Donald didn't like the way Sheldon Zemans looked at Daphne, the way he patted her shoulder. He didn't like the two of them being in the back room together. He looked at his watch.

"I haven't got all day," he said.

Joan was looking at him as if she knew perfectly well how Zemans could get under his skin. He stared back.

He looked at his watch again and went through the curtain into the back room. They were having coffee. Sheldon Zemans looked sleek and handsome, his brown eyes shining in the deeply tanned skin, the grey hair nicely cut and a little fluffy from fresh washing. Donald could imagine his dark skin against Daphne's milky white.

"Donnie," he said, "how's my favourite slum landlord?"

"Fine," Donald said. "Next week I'm going to buy the Bank of Israel."

Daphne looked up from her coffee. She was annoyed.

"Sheldon's offering to start making extra-large in one of his top lines."

"Are we going?" Donald said.

"You two love-birds got a date?" Sheldon said. "Don't let me be the fly in the ointment."

He had white teeth that showed up well against his freshly shaved cheeks. He picked up a gold pen from the table and slid it into the pocket of his lightweight summer jacket. He had two gold rings on each hand. He was perfectly turned out, and his body was solid; he must belong to a health club somewhere. Donald couldn't stop imagining that muscular swarthy body mounted on his wife's.

"I'm sure the little Vietnamese ladies in the sweat-shop must be missing you," Donald said.

"My uncle handles the factory," Sheldon said. "I look after the sales and design."

"Let me know," Daphne said, "how many of each I'd have to take to make it worth your while."

She was smiling at him.

"I will. You're a good customer, Daphne. I got to keep my customers happy."

He was leering; Donald was sure he was undressing her with his eyes.

"I'm parked illegally," Donald said.

Daphne looked at Zemans who was standing up now, setting aside the coffee cup, adjusting his jacket.

"Donald hasn't parked legally once since I married him," Daphne said.

Zemans turned to Donald and gave him the full benefit of the bright eyes and shining teeth.

"Is it true?" he said, "that you're running a tattoo parlour?"

"Yeah," Donald said. "It's true."

"Don't they spread diseases?"

"I'm careful. You run more risk going to the dentist. You should come round sometime, Sheldon. I could tattoo your telephone number on your dick. In case you leave it behind somewhere."

Zemans walked to the door of the room.

"So long, Daphne," he said. He didn't look at Donald or speak to him.

Daphne picked up the half-empty coffee cups from the table and took them into the bathroom to dump them and rinse them out. When she came back, she looked at Donald, green eyes hard and distant.

"You went too far," she said.

"I don't like finding him here pouring that slimy charm all over you like grasshopper juice."

"He's a salesman. I buy dresses from him."

"He's a lecher."

"He's not. And you shouldn't be so rude."

"He crapped on me. I just retaliated."

"What you said was too much. He's sensitive."

"I'm sensitive too."

"You sure are. You're prickly as a porcupine."

"How do porcupines make love?"

"I'm not listening to any jokes."

"You want me to leave? Forget the whole thing?"

She looked at him as if she were seriously considering it.

"Let's go," she said.

They went out through the curtain to the shop where Joan was busy sorting papers and pretending she hadn't been listening to the argument.

"I'll be back in an hour or so," Daphne said. "You want me to bring you a sandwich?"

"No," Joan said. "I'm dieting again."

"I thought you looked slimmer," Daphne said.

"Thanks."

"What's the point," Donald said when they got outside, "in having somebody working in a store for fat women who's dieting all the time?"

"Most of the women who come in the store are dieting."

"I figured that anyone who came here had given up."

"Sometimes you don't understand anything."

"You mean if they didn't diet, they'd be even fatter?"

"All women diet, whatever size they are. They just

diet. It's something women do."

Donald unlocked the door on the passenger side.

"Maybe I should drive," Daphne said.

"Why?"

"Because I still have my licence."

"Oh for Christ's sake," Donald said, "get in the car."

Someone braked and started honking at him as he pulled a U-turn out of the parking place.

"He nearly hit you," Daphne said.

"He just likes to blow his horn. You want to go to Cynthia's?"

"I guess."

"I thought you had it all planned."

Daphne had spent the evening before looking through back issues of Royal Doulton's *International Collector's Club* Magazine and dusting the figurines in the glass case, but now she sat in silence as he drove the car through the crowded streets, the whole thing spoiled because of Sheldon Zemans.

"Do you want to see the new houses?" he said.

"Some other time."

He pulled to the left to pass a stopped streetcar. A streetcar coming the other way clanged at him, but he slid back into traffic with a couple of feet to spare.

"You're driving like a lunatic," Daphne said.

"That's how I drive."

"You'll kill us both."

She was looking out the far side of the car, away from him. Donald wanted to stop the car, climb out and go back to his office by cab, but he knew Daphne well enough to know that she'd have money in her purse to get her wherever she wanted to go, and that she'd abandon the car as soon as he did, leave it to be towed away and let him worry about finding it.

Another cream and red streetcar was stopped in front of them, and what he wanted most was to step down on the gas pedal and ram the car into it.

Instead he passed illegally on the left again. This time Daphne didn't say anything, and they maintained the strained silence until they reached The China Shoppe, Cynthia Paget's store, which had the biggest collection of Doulton figurines in the city. The store was crowded with glass and china. You didn't dare turn around quickly. Everything was small and glittery and easily chipped or cracked. Cynthia herself was tiny and brittle, her face pale, haunted by dark eye-shadow and mascara.

"I've got some lovely new things," she was saying to Daphne. "Just look. Lovely, lovely things. A Yeoman of the Guard, and here's Sweet Anne, and look at this one." She pulled out a two-character scene, an eighteenth-century lady in a long dress, a suitor in green, kneeling at her feet. That was the one Daphne would buy, he was almost sure. She loved the women in long fancy dresses, the old-fashioned formality of them.

"But look here," Cynthia was saying, "look at Easter. Isn't she lovely, in her bonnet? And look at the sweet ribbons. Lovely, lovely."

Donald was irritable, hopeless. He had made her sad and angry, and now there was nothing he could do to please her. He was crude and harsh and demanding, and he had no place in her world of figurines. It was where she went to escape from him. Nothing he would ever do would make him belong in the place where she wished to be. He could offer her nothing but cash.

As he looked at all the fine-featured imaginary women in their long dresses, he was reminded of their wedding, the bridesmaids and flower girls, Daphne in her long gown. The distrust on the faces of her family every time they looked at him. The first time she had brought him home to the only-just-respectable house in Burlington, he had sensed immediately the family's feeling that he wasn't good enough for her, and to his shame, he had bragged about his stockbroker father, his brother in the provincial civil service. His words, though true enough, had sounded like lies, and Daphne's father, an accountant with a small firm, no big success story there, had sat in judgment. Donald couldn't bring himself to invite his father and Sandra to the wedding, but Arnold and Marie came and did their best for him.

He looked at the rows of crystal stemware, the flowered cups and saucers, the matched sets of dishes, and he knew that if he didn't get out, he was going to start smashing them. He pulled out his wallet and took five hundred-dollar bills out of it, walked over to where Daphne was standing and slipped the money into the pocket of the white jacket she was wearing.

"Listen, Daph," he said, "I just remembered something. I got to run. Cynthia will call you a cab."

He walked out of the store before she could speak to him, and once outside, his body gave a kind of huge shudder of relief. The white Buick Park Lane sat by the curb; it was covered with dust and mud. There was a service station not far from here, with a car wash. The swish of water, the swirling of the soap, the ponderous descent of the roaring brush that scrubbed the top of the car, the howl of the air that dried it: he'd go through that and come out clean.

"Did you come for the rent?"
"You are a month behind."

"I'm waiting for my legacy."

"You may have a long wait."

"Yes, well, soon I'll find some other way to get the money."

"Get a better job."

"I'm not sure I could, Uncle Donald."

"You only call me that when you want to annoy me."

"You are my uncle."

Julia was sitting at a long table, nothing more than a sheet of plywood nailed over two saw-horses, and she was carving a piece of wood. On the wall behind her hung a bunch of puppets, some of them in bright costumes, others just heads suspended from nails. She was twenty-four-years old and still playing with dolls.

He watched her work. She was short and heavy-bodied, like Marie, but somehow more awkward, without any of Marie's grace. The hands that hacked at the piece of pine were square and dirty, with broken nails. What did Arnold think of her? She seemed to have nothing of her father in her except this interest in art, and even that was different. Arnold's books of poems were orderly and well-printed and suitably old-fashioned. This converted parking garage that Julia used for a studio was piled with junk, an old treadle sewing-machine in a corner with rags of all colours around it, dolls hanging on the walls, a disorderly heap of tools, sabre saw, power drill, chisels, on the long table, and leaning against the far wall, a couple of paintings that looked as if they'd been done with one of the wide brushes meant for pasting wallpaper. They were both pictures of a woman with dark hair and big dark eyes.

Julia's hair was cut short and dyed a bright orange colour, and she wore a pair of overalls over a man's sport shirt. There was no bath or shower in here, and he wondered how she kept clean. Or if. The sheets on the mattress in the corner lay in a disorderly jumble.

She was unkempt, unattractive, but there was something else about her, in the brown eyes, deep-set, the odd curve down at the edge of the eye, and something too in the cheeks and nose. Her face was like a dim remembrance of his mother's face. A parody, he thought sometimes, for his mother had been slender, and quick, and bright, even a little crazed with shining, not heavy, like Julia, cynical.

"You couldn't rent this place to anybody else, could you?" Julia said.

"I could get as much for parking as I charge you."

"Funny how people love their cars," she said.

"Cars get you where you want to go, and they don't talk back."

"That's how women used to be, isn't it?"

"I doubt it."

"Weren't they taught to open their legs and shut their mouths?"

"Mostly the opposite."

Donald noticed that there was no telephone in the room. Once Julia was here, she was cut off. There didn't seem to be any place to put clothes except a small round-topped trunk at the foot of the bed.

"Where's your waitress uniform?"

"I don't keep it here. I leave it at a friend's place. When I'm finished here, I can go and get a shower and change."

She did wash.

"You want to put in a shower here?" she said.

"Not worth it for the rent I get."

"You're a hard man."

"That's right."

She went back to her carving, knife slicing into the wood.

"I worry about your father sometimes," Donald said.

"A hard man, but with a heart of gold."

"He's all on his own since Marie died."

"He's always been on his own."

"What's that mean?"

"He's an untouchable man."

"Maybe you're right. He does seem out there all alone sometimes."

"I don't know how my mother could stand it."

"She seemed happy enough."

"Happy enough. But not *too* happy."

Donald studied the two huge crude portraits on the opposite wall. The big eyes made the faces look like masks.

Was Daphne back in the store now? Maybe Sheldon Zemans had come back to sympathize with her, taken her off to a hotel room somewhere. Or if he didn't come back on his own, Daphne had phoned him to apologize for Donald's anger, and somehow one thing had led to another.

"You don't have the rent?" he said.

"Soon, Uncle, soon. It can't mean much to you, can it, with all your properties?"

"All my properties wouldn't do me a lot of good if no one paid rent on them."

He looked around the old garage, reminded himself that he owned it, that this was all his, that Julia's mess was here on sufferance. He owned it, and more than twenty other places in this city. They were registered in his name.

"Can't you do something about the will? Don't you want whatever's coming to you? It's been weeks. He must be dead."

"I got my lawyer working on it."

"And?"

"He says we should find the body. It would be a lot easier."

"But if he drowned himself, he might be half-way to Japan."

"You know how much he left you?"

"I didn't expect him to leave me anything. He hardly knows me. But my father came back from the west coast and said I was in the will. I'm tired of being broke."

"Waiting on tables, making these dolls, what do you expect?"

"I expect to be poor, but when somebody tells me there's money for me but I can't have it, it frustrates the hell out of me."

Donald looked at the puppets hanging on the wall behind the table where Julia was working. There was something hard and ugly and frightening about all the faces, eyes that protruded grotesquely, lips of some soft, heavy substance that hung from the faces. At the table, the stocky, stiff girl with his mother's face was making another of these hideous dolls. Maybe it was just as well that he and Daphne had never had children who might grow up and prove to have such things inside them.

Women were hard these days; even the Rat, funny and careless as she was, liked to play tough, but with her, it was a game.

The walls of the old garage were stained with grease, and there were cracks in the windows. He tried to imagine living here as Julia did, cooking on the little gas stove, putting across the bolt at night and going to sleep. The corner by the bed, which held a bookshelf and a night table, was the best of it. Still not much.

"You planning to stay here all winter?" he said. "It'll be cold."

"I don't know," she said. "I don't plan that long in advance."

As he worked, every now and then, over the buzz of the needle, he could hear the Rat bumping around upstairs. He'd seen her come in from work a half hour ago. If she hadn't gone out by the time he'd finished, he'd phone her, and get her to come down and watch the last scenes of *Tattoo* with him. He had it set up in the VCR.

Beneath him, in the old dentist chair, a man lay back, his eyes closed, as Donald ran the wide shading needle across his arm, turning the skin a dark shade of green. Donald knew nothing about this man, not even his name. He'd appeared at the door and said he wanted a tattoo of a bunch of roses, but one of the roses was to have a woman's face. Donald had sketched something for him, using a plate for the roses, but adding a freehand face, the woman turned slightly away, her eyes closed, her hair blending into the petals. The man stared at the sketch for a long time and then turned and looked at Donald as if Donald might be withholding something, some hidden meaning. Told it would take a couple of sessions, the man insisted that he wanted it all done immediately, even if it took two hours or more. When Donald told him two hours was worth a hundred and twenty dollars, he pulled out the long black wallet that was chained to his belt loop, took out three fifties, and put them on the work table.

Now it was almost finished. After two hours of

work, the skin must be very painful, and he was
starting to draw more blood. Donald took a large
Kleenex and patted it on the area of the tattoo, then
spread on a little more antibiotic ointment and wiped
it dry enough to work. The man didn't open his eyes.
He had a narrow face, and working this close to him,
Donald was aware of the line where his dark whiskers
began just below the cheekbone. He had wide, flared
nostrils, and thin dark lips that hung a little open. He
was so still, he might have been asleep, maybe some
sort of self-hypnosis to control the pain.

Donald moved the shading needle across his arm,
aware, as always, that if he pressed too hard, or
moved too fast, he could rip open the flesh, tear
through the skin and down into muscle like a crazed
surgeon. Jack the Ripper. He had to be dextrous and
precise; it was part of what he liked about the work. It
made him forget everything else, all the day's annoy-
ances.

He lifted the needle away and looked at the leaf he
had been shading, then once more tenderly stroked
the buzzing machine over the pale white flesh. Most
of his customers were tanned. Summer was the big
season for tattoos, when they got their clothes off,
skins browned. The man who lay beneath him, silent,
shut off, at his mercy, was very white, as if he never
saw the sun. The veins in his eyelids were thin purple
rivers. Beneath the lids, the globe of the eyes was
unmoving.

Something strange, deathly about this stillness.
White flesh beneath the fingers of the pale disposable
rubber gloves that Donald wore to work. He was very
careful. He didn't want to give diseases or catch them.

AIDS. That lethal invisible corruption of the blood.

A couple more passes with the wide shading needle

and it would be completed. Thirty-six hundred times a minute the needle oscillated back and forth to insert the coloured dye under the epidermis. In a drawer somewhere Donald had a crude homemade needle that someone had made in prison, the drive of a tape player, with a metal loop soldered on one edge so that as the spindle turned, the needle was pulled back and forth through the barrel of a ball-point pen.

"OK. You're all done." Donald put a piece of gauze over the surface to pick up the last of the blood that was oozing out in a couple of spots. He rubbed some of the antibiotic ointment over the whole surface of the tattoo. The man examined it.

"That what you wanted?"

"Yeah."

"We'll put some gauze over it for now. You may get a little more blood."

Donald taped the gauze then pulled off his gloves and threw them in the garbage and reached in his pocket for the three fifty-dollar bills. His back and neck were a bit stiff from working so long in one position.

"A hundred and twenty," he said, then stashed the bright pink bills in his wallet and handed the man three tens.

"Lots of soap and water for the next day or so."

The man didn't speak. He was out the door and gone, and the place was suddenly and ominously quiet, the only sound the traffic from the Danforth half a block away. The gloves lay limp in the plastic garbage pail, like pieces of a lost body that had been turned transparent by an uncontrolled burst of radiation.

Donald heard footsteps cross the floor above him, a soft impact at each step, the Rat walking across the bedroom in her bare feet. He remembered the flat white toes, the hollow just below the ankle, the way the muscles of the leg curved away from the framework of bone. Her eyes. The way the thin, straight blonde hair grew forward at the temple.

He put the needles in some solvent and turned them on to wash themselves clean. In a few minutes he'd drop them in the sterilizer. Or maybe it was better to wait until morning. The sterilizer was starting to overheat. If he let it run dry, it could start a fire and burn the place down.

Overhead, the Rat moved again, away from the bed, toward her kitchen. Donald was remembering the thin, colourless down that grew at the top of the spine, how it felt against his tongue.

He dialled the telephone. Heard it ring overhead.

"Hello."

"Rat. Come down and see a movie."

"Why don't you come up?"

"Maybe later."

She didn't answer, just hung up. He threw away the used capsules of ink and wiped the table clean with a paper towel.

He'd pocket the three fifty-dollar bills without recording them. Maybe he'd use the cash to take Daphne out to dinner later on. If she hadn't run off with Sheldon.

He heard the Rat's footsteps on the stairs, and she walked past the front window of the store. Her legs were bare and she wore a man's white shirt with a black belt around it. Donald met her at the door, to lock it and turn the sign to Closed, and as she passed by, she reached up and gave him a soft little kiss on the mouth.

"You look good, Rat," he said.

"What's this movie we're going to watch?"

"I told you. *Tattoo.*"

"You have a thing about that movie."

"I just want to show you the part at the end."

"And then you think I'm going to let you draw all over me."

"Maybe someday. Go sit down."

Donald turned on the TV set and took the remote control back to his tattooing stool. The Rat was sitting in the dentist chair with her feet drawn up, hugging her legs and staring at the screen. "The Newlywed Game" appeared and the MC started to babble.

"Let's watch," she said. "I like it when one of the guys says something really dumb and you can see the wife start to get mad and then she remembers she's on TV and she gets all sweet again and you know as soon as they're out of there, it'll be the biggest fight you ever saw."

"You like to see them fight?"

"Yeah."

"Well we're here to watch this movie."

Donald pressed the button on the remote control and the VCR gave a little click and the picture changed. The film began.

"What's he doing?" the Rat said.

"He's just finishing a tattoo with that red flower on her thigh."

"She's letting him do that? Tattoo all over her?"

"No. That's what the movie's about. He kidnaps her."

"He's a freak. Bruce Dern always plays freaks."

"But the tattoos are beautiful on her. Look."

"Her whole back's covered with those big blue flowers. What's that on her belly?"

"It's some kind of a heron. Look at the yellow

plumage. Beautiful."

"That's freaky. Who's the actress?"

"Maude Adams."

"She's got a nice body. Skinny, but her tits are bigger than mine. I'm glad he didn't tattoo all over them."

"Just that little bit of foliage to make them part of the design."

"Christ, look, *he's* covered with designs too."

"He got tattooed by some Jap at the beginning of the movie."

"Are they going to screw?"

"Yes. It's great, with all the tattoos."

"What are you trying to do to me, Donald? Showing me fuck movies. I get turned on just looking at the packages of safes out at the store."

"With all those tattoos, you can't tell one body from the other."

"It's like two great big snakes."

"See how all the patterns are moving. All the colours."

"Christ."

"You can almost feel the skin."

"That's his back, with the dragon. Look at it moving. Christ, Donald, this is too much."

"She kills him at the end."

"Why?"

"She doesn't want to come."

"That's crazy."

"Because he kidnapped her and forced her to get tattooed."

"Is she going to do it with that tattooing needle?"

"Yes."

Donald didn't much want to watch the murder, so he pressed the button, and the machine stopped with a click and a whirr, and "The Newlywed Game" reappeared with a huge burst of metallic laughter. He turned off the TV. When he turned around, the Rat was staring at him. It roused and frightened him when she looked at him like that, the face so hot and bare, the eyes naked and shining.

"What did you think of it, Rat?"

"Let's go upstairs," she said. "OK?"

"OK, Rat. Let's go."

He switched off the lights, and the two of them went to the door of the shop and past the window to the stairway. The Rat pulled out her key and opened the door.

"You were right about that. It's fantastic," she said.

"Most of it isn't that great. Just the beginning and the end. Sometime I'll show you the beginning, a bunch of tattooed Japs in loin-cloths."

They were walking up the stairs. Donald reached out and touched her and she stopped, looked toward him, put her hand against his lips. Then she opened the door and they were inside. Donald always expected her place to be a mess, but she kept it neat.

Without a word she went to the wide bed, and in a couple of seconds she'd peeled off her clothes and lay waiting for him.

"Come on, Duck," she said. "Get in here."

Donald stood beside the bed and undressed.

"You're the only guy I know who isn't circumcised," she said.

"My father didn't believe in it."

"Why not?"

"I don't really know."

"Funny little spout."

"I suppose."

"I once heard that uncircumcised guys give you

cancer."

"I heard they give you a better time."

"Show me, Duck."

He kissed her and felt the pressure of her protruding teeth against his lips.

"You're so wet."

"You make me excited, Donald."

She was digging her long fingernails into his back.

"No marks, Rat. I told you before, no marks."

"You got too many rules, Donald. You don't give a girl half a chance."

Her hands slid up over his skin and her fingers buried themselves in his hair. Her legs were locked together over his back. Her hands gripped tight, pulling his hair, and he felt her shudder against him.

"More," she said, "more."

7

When you told me that you were going away, and for so long, abandoning me, I said, you suggested that I might write things down, a journal, a long desultory letter, that I could imagine your presence at the end of the couch and talk to you. After all, during my appointment, my weekly hour, I don't see you there, do I? There are times when you are silent, only a listening ear. Once when I was talking, something about Arnold and Donald, how I couldn't believe these little boys were really my sons, my own sons, I thought all of a sudden that you had disappeared in some magical fashion, been transported away, and I was alone in the room, talking to myself. What I was saying evaporated, sizzled to nothing like a drop of water on a hot griddle, and all I could think was that I must look around to find you there. I strained my ears to hear the sound of your breathing but I couldn't. I was sure you were gone, but too proud to turn and look, and too stupid with fear to invent a question that you would answer and prove to me your existence. I lay there, suddenly unable to hear anything, unable to speak, paralyzed by anxiety, dismay. When you spoke, asking me to go on, at first I couldn't hear you. I was deaf with fear, until at last you touched my shoulder to get my attention, and it all fell away like a cape tossed aside in a warm room. You were with me, after all, even when I had lost my awareness of you. You were there, listening.

Another day, I imagined you as a giant ear, an ear the size of a man, an ear that could contain all the stories I told, all the stories from the appointment before mine and the appointment after. The Listener. What is needed for this talking cure.

And how I do talk, how I do go on talking. As here, as now. I bought a lovely leather-bound notebook to write to you, and I keep it close to me. I think that I will be different while I have this book than I would be without it. Different memories, different images, different feelings will arrive because the book is here to record them.

What, I thought, lying in bed last night, if you were never to return? Panic, panic, and I had to get up. But then I thought that still I would talk to you in this book, for all the rest of my life, perhaps, I would have you as my listener, and because you were present to listen, words would come. You are at the head of the couch, invisible, but all-powerful in your silent evocation of what is inside me. When I write in this book, you are there, listening.

But ask no questions. No clever, sly, insidious questions appearing so innocent and then turning the world on its head. The book cannot ask those questions, and in that way (dreadful, I don't want to think this), it will not be you. Nothing will be the same.

You say you will come back. You have promised me, and all your patients, that you will return after this trip, this pilgrimage to London, where the Professor died in exile, this trip to meet his daughter, to see the place where his ashes rest, that wise old Jew. He is, to put it in a form of words, the only Jew I have ever known. They are there, in parts of the city, furriers, tailors, merchants, but we do not meet them. Toronto is not Vienna. If we have wise Jews like the Professor, they are wise in the isolation of their own neighbourhoods. They practise an alien religion, and some of them are bearded and strange, and they carry the pain of all those relatives killed in the concentration camps. There are pictures, but I do not look at them. I do not have the strength. I tried to ignore the war, because when I thought of it, I thought it would go on forever and it would come and take my sons, even though they were only babies.

Now it is over, and you have found a way to travel to England, to search for the spirit of the Professor among the wreckage. Did you take parcels of food? They are so poor there, after the war, after the bombing, at least I hear that is so. You say you will come back. You expect to come back. This is only a kind of holiday, an opportunity for spiritual refreshment, a chance to think new thoughts. In a new place, to think new thoughts. I too am in a new place, having no regular hour at which to see you, but having instead this book in which I will talk to you. The whole shape of my life will be altered, for the book is always here, but the week will not shape itself around the regular times, every other hour being an hour before or an hour after.

So there you are at the end of the couch, unseen, a

presence, a giant ear listening, listening. And I will bring you a dream. A dream which is a memory. Or a memory redreamed, brought back from the unconscious in the mystery of sleep. Or shall I tell you the memory? It is a true memory. I know how it happened, just how. And in the dream, it was the same. Perhaps this was a dream of wishing to return, longing to go back, because in the dream I was young and I thought I was safe (though there is pain too), but perhaps that is the great mistake, looking back, to think that those things were safe, only because they are past and have the stillness of the past. In the memory I weep, and in the dream, I did not weep.

Why didn't I weep in the dream? Where had I lost my tears? Am I a dust-bowl, like the prairie in a season of drought? My brother Leonard crossed the prairie in the days of the terrible drought, and when he came back, he couldn't describe it. He said it was too terrible to speak of. I didn't cry in the dream. As if I were a land in the grip of a drought, a dust-bowl. The well is dry or the well is full; one bucket finds water, another comes up empty. I am both parched and rich with the tumbling water of rivers, weeping in memory, dry in the dream.

Are you listening? No. You are in England. You have gone off to seek the death of the wise Jew. One day I wished to go to the neighbourhood where they live, the Jews, and seek out one and ask him the mystery of where the Professor became wise, he who brought back news from the land of the dead, from the lost aeons when the tribes wandered in the desert or clustered at an oasis. That was the best part of Sunday School, those old stories of the desert tribes, the long garments in the pictures, the fierce simplicity of the tales, Jacob and Joseph and Saul and David. The best stories were those in which God spoke to a child or a man alone. *Saul has slain his thousands, and David his ten thousands.* No. Not those. Stories of kings rivalrous, and much killing. No. Not those, but the miracles of the child hearing the voice of God, water flowing in the desert. Sunday, freshly pressed blouse and middie, and those stories.

The book is to invoke your presence. I open it in front of me. Let me imagine that I am waiting in the house, that I have made arrangements for Mary to be here with the boys, and that I have phoned a taxi and it has driven me to that house on St Clair.

There is a lawn with a small hedge, and a brass plate beside the door, and when I reach the door with the brass plate, I want to slow down. Until now I have been rushing, determined, but now I wish to proceed slowly, because once the hour is begun, too soon it will be over, so as I go up the stairs, I move with a certain deliberation, and at the top, I open the door to the waiting room, as if I had all the time in the world and could not quite imagine what might be on the other side, and had only a passing interest in finding out. Once inside, I study the paintings on the walls, two of them, more modern, more jagged than I am used to seeing, one a kind of city, all darkness and light, all rising edges and flashing illuminations, and the other pale and brilliant, an evocation of mountains and snow and solitude, and as I sit waiting for my hour to commence, I wonder why you have chosen those paintings, what you expected them to evoke, whether you might distinguish your patients by what they see, by which they choose to stare at. From hour to hour, I choose differently, but whichever I choose, I study, carefully, almost fixedly, as a kind of preparation for seeing you.

Finally the door will open, and the previous appointment comes out. We nod, but do not speak. He is a tall young man, with very straight light brown hair, very well dressed in a dark brown, three-piece suit. I try not to speculate about him; it seems unfair. But he looks to me like a young man that Ross might meet through his work, the son of a large business family, or a young banker.

Then I am inside. I never notice that I open the door or how I pass through, only that I am inside and in your presence, and that somehow I have closed the door behind me, and that you are in your chair, or perhaps across the room, putting something in place on the wide table that serves you as a desk, the wide beautiful table with curving legs and a ball and claw foot. Lying on the couch, I become fascinated by that foot, by the idea that there is a wild beast caught in the table, like an animal in a fairy-tale who has been turned into wood, and all the fierceness of that animal is imprisoned in the tight curve of that leg, in the grasp of those claws on the wooden ball of the foot.

You look at me, and greet me, in your polite way, and indicate the couch and then you have disappeared; you are behind me; you are the giant ear that is waiting to hear whatever it is that I have to present.

So, now, I put you there, and I bring you my memory, my dream. Summer. This is a memory of summer. In summer, we lived in the country, all of us sometimes, and sometimes only mother and Leonard and I, with a local girl who helped out, Gladys Joiner her name was, while my father stayed in the city and went on with his medical practice, his unmarried sister, Zena, moving into our house to cook for him. The day I'm remembering, my father was staying at the cottage with us, and Gladys Joiner, who was something of a tyrant when he was away, had been driven back to her proper role. My mother was a little afraid of Gladys, but Gladys was immensely in awe of my father because he was a doctor. She would ask me to tell her how he cut people open and took things out, and though I knew nothing about medicine or surgery, I would try to put on a professional manner and answer her.

There is so much to remember. The dream, the memory, is perhaps only a moment, but behind it, all around it, the other presences move like distant bright stars. How much is to be told about Gladys Joiner, whose greatest wish, I believe, was to undergo surgery at my father's hands, preferably some calamitous major operation, and then perhaps to have the excised part stored in a jar in formaldehyde and to be forever-after something of a cripple, with the lost organ close at hand for study, to be offered as an explanation of her sickly state. She had, on her soft white belly, a small growth, and one day she showed it to me. She wondered if she ought to consult my father on the possibility of having it cut off. A little knob of loose flesh, harmless, I suspected, and told her so, glad to use my privileged status as the doctor's daughter to give advice to Gladys Joiner. I don't know if she ever approached my father for a more professional diagnosis of this growth and its surgical possibilities, but I know how often, as I saw her working in the kitchen, or as she walked along the dusty road to the store with me and Leonard, I would imagine the white flesh, and the little superfluous knob.

Not an accident, either, that memory, not just a childish intrusion, for there is a connection, some-where, a connection to the birds. The shock of life invaded by something unsuitable, a tiny horror. You have taught me to make these connections. Every drop of water runs from the cold springs far underground.

We were all there, at the cottage, my mother and father in their room, Leonard in his, I in mine, and down the road was the Joiner's house, where Gladys lived. The night had passed, a wakeful, hot, moonlit, haunted night, full of strange noises. In the middle of the night, I lay on my side in bed, and saw a square of moonlight cast on the floor and felt myself a fairy-tale waif, alone and fearful of the moon's cold magic. I climbed from my bed and stood in that patch of moonlight, shaking, although the night was warm. The world was so far off, and even those around me, my parents, my brother, were foreign and uncomforting. Outside the window, my mother's garden was colourless and strange, odd and hurtful black shapes where in daylight there were gifts of red and yellow and mauve. I returned to bed, and the night passed, and I woke into bright early sunlight. The first awake, I pulled on clothes and walked on tiptoe past the door of my parents' bedroom and out into the screened porch where we ate and where we often sat in the evenings.

After the troubled, almost sleepless night, my vision was a little blurred, as if my head might be filled with smoke or mist. I stood and looked across the garden, and took in the colours of the lemon lilies, the bed of roses, the morning glory that climbed up a pole just outside the porch, and I was only half-aware, at first, of something on the screen, something there. And there. And there. I was slow to take it in, slow to walk closer, but then quick to find myself in tears, biting back a scream. The things, the tiny undefined shapes on the screen were humming-birds. We watched them as they came to the garden, the quick hovering presences, tiny as bees, that fed on the nectar of my mother's flowers, shiny green with a splash of ruby at the neck. The fine beaks delicately entered the throat of a flower, the wings beating so fast to hold the bird still in the air that they were only a blur, and then suddenly they would dart away. For some reason, some illusion of sound or scent, three of the lovely miniscule things had put their beaks through the screen and been trapped there, and now the bodies, hardly bigger than my thumb, hung limp and dead on the screen. I ran out of the porch, crying, my body all jangled with the horror of it. It was as if, in the night, as I stood there, crazed in the moonlight, I had drawn them to me, as if I had been the flower that called them to their destruction. I was curled in a chair, still crying, when my mother found me, and at first, when I couldn't bear to show her, she thought it was just one of my moods, and she was a little angry, and my father came too, prepared to be impatient, and finally, not looking, I led them to the porch, and insisted they examine the screen, and then my mother saw, and gave a little sound and pointed them out to my father who went outside, and then they were gone.

Where had they gone? At the time, I didn't or wouldn't think of that question, but in the dream, that became, somehow, of the greatest importance, the thing I had to know. After it was over (it, what was it?), I was standing in the porch, and I was looking at the screens in the places where the little soft bodies of the dead birds had been and I was trying to think where they had gone, almost as if I wished them to be back there. As if they had been stolen from me, as if I had been deprived of them somehow. My father had buried them or simply thrown them into the long grass, removing them. As he had operated on so many people, taking out tonsils, appendix, uterus, pieces of infected flesh. I was afraid that he had, without my knowledge, operated on Gladys Joiner and removed that growth, and now she kept it in a jar. It was dreadful to me that all these things were happening without my knowledge, behind my back. In the dream, I thought *behind my back*, and turned around and Ross was there with my two boys, Arnold and Donald, and I was happy to see them, but then I realized that now the screen, the birds, my father, Gladys Joiner, were invisible, now they were *behind my back*. No matter which way I turned, there were secrets, and I was helpless in their midst. Do something, I tell myself in the dream. Find those little birds. But I didn't want to turn away from Ross and my boys, even though *behind my back*, my father was doing something to the birds. I began to suspect— suspicion is the poisoned air of dreams—that during that mad moonlit night, he had somehow caused the death of the humming-birds, as a demonstration of his power over me, over the natural world, the power of the surgeon with his knife, the power that Gladys Joiner worshipped so devoutly.

It was in that state of confusion, torn between secrets, knowing that there would always be something dangerous behind me, that I woke, confused, for a moment, as so often, about where I was, listening for Ross's breathing, looking for the light that comes in at the edge of the bedroom curtains, lying very still until I could gather the dispersed atoms of myself into a person again. Then remembered, astonished, that those little boys in the dream were real, that Arnold and Donald were asleep in their rooms. But were they? Why did I believe that my dream had damaged them? Quietly, I slipped out of the bed and walked down the hall to the rooms where they slept, to see them, to reach out and gently touch them with my fingertips, feel them warm and alive, Arnold with an arm thrown out to one side, his face turned away, Donald curled in a tight little ball.

Does that finish my hour? Must I return next week to explore the meanings of that dream? Will you ask me for my associations to bird, flesh, knife, moonlight? No, because you have run away from me, abandoned me. You are in England on a pilgrimage to the last earthly home of the wise doctor. Once I had a longing to find my way to Vienna and see that handsome, bearded face, to hear that voice. Then he was in London, and there was a war, and I was the mother of sons who must be protected. Then he was dead, the good doctor, the wise listener who could take into himself the most terrible fears, and only by listening and asking and again listening, could see them made harmless.

I suppose my hour is over, and I must rise from the couch and leave, and on the way out, see the next appointment, the very tall woman, so severe, in a hat and veil, "the woman in mourning" is how I think of her, and we nod, as we always do, and I go out to the street, and perhaps stop at a restaurant for tea before finding a taxi to take me home, where the house, strangely, is unchanged by my journey into night and dream, the noise of my sons playing is heard from the yard, and when I am inside, I take off my coat and my hat and hang them in the closet in the front hall, and come into the front room, and everything is in place, the rich colours of the carpet, the wing chair where Ross sits at night with his newspaper, the Victorian chair where I sit, and on the sideboard, the delicate

Venetian glass goblets which we bought on our honeymoon in that dream city.

Because you are not here, I can talk to you anytime.
Which, perhaps, is never, but I go on, as if you might
read this, as if you were there at the end of the couch.
The days go by. The weeks. You will return, and you
will have seen the urn holding the ashes of the old
man. At a party once, a woman told me a dreadful
story about him, at the end, in the last days, that the
cancer that ate away his face made him stink, the
smell so strong that a favourite dog cowered away
from him. I refused to believe it and yet a part of me
knew it must be true. Such a bald, bad joke as life
would play.

I stare at the delicate goblets that we brought home
from our honeymoon. That dream city, Venice, the city
of glass and gold and water. I have always been
frightened of water. It angered my Father that I would
not learn to swim, but I couldn't bear the cold embrace, the terror of losing my breath. So many fears. It
was on the boat that took us to Europe that Ross said
to me, that first night, "Are you frightened?" and
made everything possible. He was handsome and
upright and manly, and I knew he would do well in
the world, but once I was pledged to marry him, I was
apprehensive about what he would do to me, but
once he had asked that, I could tell him and tremble,
in his arms, and when we reached Venice, we were all
golden for each other. I thought that my body was
made of chips of gold and shining rock like the
mosaics in San Marco.

Gold and fire and water. I dreamed myself into
such a state of grace that when we crossed the long

stretch of water to Murano, the island of the glass-blowers, I held his hand and believed that we were flying through the air, not floating inches from the dark possibility of drowning. And we saw: the blinding light of the furnace where the molten glass was a bowl of yellow incandescence, the glass-blowers twisting and shaping and carving the heavy fluid glass into the perfect shapes of cups and glasses and table ornaments, the delicate twisted stems of the goblets we would bring home. And we saw: a little tree with dark green fruit that I could not recognize. Figs. The bright-painted boats, the houses at the edge of the canal, the precarious existence of this little island in the sea.

In Venice we were always lost. I wouldn't let Ross buy a map, and we did not speak the language. It was so mysterious and wonderful that life went on here in foreign sounds, men and women talking in what might have been the songs of birds for all I understood of it. We could not comprehend the language, and we had no map, so we were always lost, and would walk for hours down little streets, wandering into blind squares, coming back to cross a little bridge and look along the *rio* to see a glimpse of the Grand Canal at the end, and then turn and come on a church or palace, and follow a street beyond and stop in exhaustion at a wine shop, to point at the food and offer money, trusting the merchants to take only the right price and hardly caring if we were cheated. Afterward, we would come out of the little shop, and a gondola would appear and then vanish, under a bridge, into a narrow waterway, gone. We walked until, worn out, we found familiar alleys and squares and the doorway of the hotel where they spoke a little

English, and we would fall into each other's arms, and we were young and golden and holy as all the ancient churches, and delicate as Venetian lace.

Such a place as Venice does not exist. It was a dream that I invented when Ross asked me "Are you frightened?" and I could answer, and almost lose my fear.

The question is, Why, when I can remember all that beauty, do I believe that I am dying? Perhaps they are related, happiness and this weary belief in the closeness of death. I have been to all the doctors, and they assure me that they can find no disease, but I know that my body is not working properly. There is this and that and this and that. Take my lungs, for example. It is harder to breathe than it should be. Other people, I know, breathe without an effort, without counting the seconds of air taken in, wondering if this breath will be enough.

There is not enough of me to live a whole life. I am too scant. My being is stretched too tight. All through the war, I tried to avoid seeing the newspapers, hearing the discussions. I was too weak to contain a war. It startled me that Ross could discuss it, could hold opinions on the military strategy, the political consequences. All I could see was that they were killing young boys, and that one day they would come for mine, that the sweet white flesh of their small bodies would be shot by bullets, burst with explosives. They are so young, even Arnold, though he is so beautifully serious and concerned to be an adult, though the child keeps trying to break through, in laughter, in wild plans for the future. And Donald, so watchful, so brave, though he was little more than a baby, insisting on going to school alone even the first day.

Yes, they say the war is over, but there will always

be another one. That is the way of it. When we went to Venice for our honeymoon, they told us that Mussolini was a force for good, that he had turned the Italian rabble into a disciplined modern civilization. Then he was the enemy, and at the end, there were terrible pictures of his body hanging dead, mocked and insulted.

None of it makes any sense to me. Is there something wrong with me, or is there something too much shy of perfection in the whole business of living? I am not a good citizen. I am not a good mother and wife. I am all in tatters. I can't get enough breath in my lungs, and in front of my eyes, the atoms of matter will not hold still. Sometimes I think it is something created by the atom bomb, by all those tests we read of and by the bombs they dropped on Japan. Sometimes it seems to me that they have tampered with the nature of matter, and now, for some of us, it will never again be still, but always in motion, as if each of the colours of the world were a million tiny wriggling worms.

Will the world ever again be still?

Some of these things I have written are things I could not tell you, even if you were there, in the room with me, the plant on its table nearby, the water-colour of rolling treeless hills observing us, you invisible behind me. I don't think that I have ever told you that since the atom bomb, the colours of the world are little wriggling worms of light. Nor ever asked what was happening in Venice when, somewhere in Italy, they hung Mussolini's body by the feet. Was the city still golden, still a dream, a joke played by men on the sea?

This book affects me oddly. It draws words from me. At first, it was to be my hour with you, regular, helpful, an event that gave a shape to my week, and so to each day. But now it is always with me, and in the middle of the night, when I lie awake, I begin to scribble, in the privacy of my dark brain. It has become an addiction. Soon perhaps I will carry it everywhere with me, and in the middle of a meal, will draw it out and begin to write. I said that there was not enough of me to live, and yet, at the same time, there is too much of me, I can never get it all down.

The book is my secret. I haven't told Ross about it, and I keep it hidden in a drawer under my clothes, although I can't explain why it's so secret. I've written nothing to shock or shame him, but still I can't let it out. Just as I don't tell him, after I have come back from seeing you, what I have said, so I have no way of telling him what I have written here.

Has anyone ever suggested that we are created by our secrets? That only what is secret is truly our own?

Like the birth of children. When I was pregnant, my sons were entirely mine, even when they began to move on their own, even when my body grew huge and was buffeted from within by earth tremors, rolling seas, wrestling matches. Still the living creature was my baby. It was within me. Ross had his moment of injection, and afterward it was all mine. But then they were torn from me, in pain and blood, and no matter how I hold them to me, my sons are no longer my own. They are growing boys. They imitate their father and the other men they see. They are tiny citizens of a country. They are like words spoken on a platform in front of a crowd, gone.

Sometimes when I look at them, I know that they can read on my face the terrible mother's hunger to hold them close and keep them safe. To keep them, my secrets. Impossible. They too have abandoned me,

and without them, there is less of me, and already
there was not enough. If they would only stay close
enough to me, I could be adequate. I could be a good
mother. But they go away, they leave me bereft, and
suddenly I am all transparent and hopeless. They
have abandoned me by being born, by growing up.
Now you have abandoned me, and I have had to
replace you by this book, which turns out to be
something altogether different. I can no longer con-
vince myself that I am in your room, lying on the
couch, telling you things. This book was addressed to
you, but now, it has become some other listener. I am
as unfaithful, perhaps, as all the rest of the world.
When you aren't there to listen to me, I lose you. Try
then to imagine you, where you are, in a grim city, a
grey city in ruins, something I have concocted out of
photographs. So I place you, remembered, imagined,
in this city of ruins, and among the broken buildings,
the rubble of ruined houses, you make your visit to
the ashes of Freud.

Why does the dream of the humming-birds come
back? What is its power? For many years, they vanished, one memory among so many others, but now
they have come back to haunt me. I think it has
something to do with my boys, my sense of their
helplessness, like the helplessness of the small beautiful birds, betrayed by a sound or odour. In the dream
last night, Gladys Joiner had found the bodies of the
birds, and she had taken them out of the screen to
make into a pie, but she complained that there were
not enough, and that I must be sent out in the woods
for more. They grew on long stalks, like raspberries,
and as they hung there, they were alive, but unable to
fly, and their eyes regarded me fearfully as my hands

reached out to pick them for Gladys Joiner's pie. I could not bring myself to pluck these pretty trapped birds, for I knew that as soon as they were snatched from the stalk, they would die, dozens of them would die in my hands. I turned to run, but wherever I looked, there were more of the stalks, more bright panicky eyes.

I woke, and Ross was not in bed. I was alone. At first I was paralyzed, alone and convinced I would be alone forever, that Ross had been taken by some bad miracle, or that he had never been there, that I had wakened from a dream of marriage into the truth of solitude. I could not move, and my breath would not come without the most concentrated effort. I had to count each breath. If I lost count, I would asphyxiate and die. So I breathed and counted, and very carefully, I moved my eyes across the room and took in its silence and emptiness. The shape of the heavy drapes, the dim light shining through the drawn blind, the tassles on the valance. If I could see those, it would be better, I was convinced of that.

Finally I was able to move my hand, to lift it and touch my face, feel the warm breath that came out of my lungs. I didn't need to concentrate so hard on the mere task of drawing oxygen into my body. I was able to turn my head to see the dark corners of the room, where someone might be hiding, in wait, to fall on me or bring me the bad message I dreaded. By the time I was close to a thousand breaths, I was able to stop counting, and even to climb out of bed, put on my dressing-gown and walk out of the bedroom.

I discovered Ross downstairs, at a table, with a pencil and paper, scribbling figures. In my relief, I found that my eyes were wet, but I wiped them and promised myself that I would be brave and only say that I had wakened and come looking for him and should I make Ovaltine for us both?

8.

Driving through Victoria, after the funeral, on their way back to Sandra's house, Arnold had seen an old Chinese woman, bent, wearing dark trousers and a hat, and with a long stick on her shoulder, like something from a photograph in *National Geographic*, except that on the end of the stick were not the traditional wicker baskets, but plastic carrying bags. It was a kind of cross-cultural pun that seemed to demand explication, interpretation. Then they turned a corner, and the woman was gone, and Arnold wondered if he had imagined her. Was she some gloss on his dilettante interest in China, offered by an unconscious stirred up by the huge fact of his father's funeral?

"I was surprised to see you here, Donald," Sandra said.

"So was I," Donald answered.

"Daphne couldn't come?"

"No."

Now that the others were gone, the three of them sat together, as if waiting for some final message, some final symbolic act that would release them.

"I'm glad you came," Sandra said. "Ross always regretted not seeing more of you."

"These things happen."

"You were very angry."

"I was a kid. Kids see the world differently."

Donald remembered even now the scene in the large dim living-room of their house in Rosedale, his father, stiffly, coldly marching through the announcement that he was leaving them. His mother was shut in her room upstairs. Donald had been seized, first, by a terror, that came on him as vertigo, a sickness that swelled inside his brain while he clung to the chair he sat in, struggling not to faint or vomit, and then, after he had run from the room, from the house, the fear was gradually mixed with a frantic rage, and he swore, speaking aloud, as if to some recording angel, as he lay hidden behind the hedge of a little park, that he would kill his father, would find a weapon and shed his blood. Then he began to cry, unable to understand why his father would abandon them, would strip their lives of all sense and order. At the time Donald ran from the room, his father's stern voice shouting at him that he must come back, there had been no explanation of why he was leaving, and it was only later that Arnold would tell him that it was for another woman who would replace their mother in his life, and when Donald heard this, he refused at first to believe it, then swore if any such unthinkable woman should exist, he would kill her too.

Opposite him, Sandra was sitting in the corner of a soft couch, one leg folded under the knee of the other, a youthful posture that belied the signs of age, wrinkles, puffiness, on her face.

"Are you going to stay in this house?" Arnold said.

"For the time being. I have a few friends here, though there's nobody very close. My best friend and her husband moved to Florida two years ago. My brother and his wife are there too. Probably I'll go down for a while this winter. Maybe I'll want to settle there, but I might not be able to get a visa."

"You could spend the winters there," Arnold said. "Buy a condo and sit by the pool with the other widows."

Donald looked across the room, at the cool slender figure of his father's second wife. What, he wondered, was the source of that easy elegance? Was it something she had always possessed, one of the things his father had wanted, wanted enough to abandon his first, once precious, wife? Or was it something Sandra had learned through all the years of comfortable living, plenty of money and no children? So controlled, so fleshless. Yet this was the woman who had excited his father so intensely that he had chosen to leave his family for her. Had she then gone cold on him, become this picture of fashionable restraint?

"So we'll go into Victoria in the morning to see the lawyer?" Arnold said.

"Will you come by for me?" Sandra said.

"We'll pick you up here at nine-thirty."

"I'll be glad when it's over, first the funeral, now the will. After all these weeks of waiting, being in limbo."

"I didn't believe he was dead," Donald said.

"I knew he was, but I couldn't let myself learn to live with it because there was still the slight chance that he might walk in the door."

"They *were* sure about the identification?"

"Yes."

"Is there anything we can do for you, before we go back to the motel?" Arnold said.

"No. But having you here for the funeral was very helpful. Having you both here."

"I still don't believe he's dead," Donald said.

"They were sure, Donald. The clothes, the dental work."

"I know that, but I don't believe it."

"You hadn't seen him for a long time," Arnold said. "He'd become like something you'd imagined, not someone real who could die and vanish."

"A lot of people at the funeral," Donald said.

"Ross was a popular man," Sandra said, "but still I was a little surprised that so many showed up after all the confusion of his disappearance, when it took this long to find the body."

"Perhaps it made people more aware of it. A whole story, not just an event," Arnold said.

"Perhaps," Sandra said. Donald thought she sounded a little impatient with Arnold's theorizing. He looked over at her, and their eyes met, and something passed between them. It startled him that he was suddenly aware of her as a human being, a woman. He didn't like it. Didn't like it at all. Things should stay in their place. He didn't want to understand her or to understand his father. Things should stay in their place. He tapped his hand against the edge of a table, and the rhythmic activity seemed to fuel his restlessness.

"Should I be offering you something?" Sandra said.

"A drink? Coffee?"

"It's probably time for us to go," Arnold said. Bill and Stephanie from next door had helped them clean up the dishes left by the small crowd who had come to the house after the burial. Arnold sensed that Donald was getting restive and agitated.

"We'll be back in the morning," he said.

Outside the house, he walked to the driver's door of the car that he and Donald had rented at the airport.

"You're driving, are you?" Donald said.

"Yes," Arnold said. "I have a licence."

The motel parking lot was crowded with the cars of people who were drinking in the bar.

"Want to get a drink?" Donald said.

"Yes."

The doorway of the bar was blocked by a young couple who were kissing enthusiastically, the tall young man's neck bent forward and pressed into the face of the blonde girl, her fingers gnawing at the small of his back like hungry little animals. Something about these scrabbling hands made Donald think of the Rat. Too many things made him think of the Rat. Last night, in the motel bed, he had found himself imagining her there with him.

"Lots of room in the parking lot," Donald said, and the two broke apart, stared at the two men without speaking, and walked off into the night in a love-drugged silence. Inside, the sound of the band echoed off the walls and assaulted the ears.

"I'm not sure I can stand this," Arnold said, but Donald had found an empty table, and by the time they sat down, the band had finished and announced a break before the next set. A tape was turned on, slightly less loud.

The waitress who came to their table was blunt and breezy. She took their order and vanished.

"We're the oldest people in the room," Arnold said.

"Maybe there's some other bar here for old guys from the motel. Or maybe we're supposed to hide out in our rooms with a bottle."

"I don't know how long I can stand the noise."

A tall dark girl walked by their table in a very short skirt.

"There are all these beautiful young bodies to look at," Donald said.

The people in the bar all seemed to know each other, shouted back and forth from one table to another. Arnold sat and waited for his drink, unattached to anything here, a spectator, in attendance at the noise of life.

"I was on a roof the other day," Donald was saying, "with some patching compound. In the evening. It was too hot to work up there during the day. There was some kind of leak in the upstairs apartment of this place, so I went up to patch all the flashing, anything else I could see that might need it. Kind of nice night. The leaves were blowing a bit, not too hot, and down in the street, I saw these two old guys go past, one of them with a cane, and all of a sudden, I wanted to jump off the roof. Just jump."

"Why?"

"No reason."

The waitress brought their drinks. Arnold paid.

"You should stop climbing on roofs," Arnold said.

The girl in the short skirt came back past the table. Donald watched her.

"Don't they drive you crazy?" he asked his brother. "All these beautiful young girls."

"They're nice to look at. Like young animals or

beautiful flowers."

"You don't want to touch them, every one of them?"

"I can resist it."

Donald looked across the room to where the girl was sitting. The man with her had a round, almost effeminate face.

"They're dangerous," he said.

"Who?"

"Women. They can do things to you."

"Are you having an affair?" Arnold said.

"You could call it that."

"That have anything to do with wanting to jump off the roof?"

"No."

"You've had other women before now, haven't you?"

"A poke now and then. Nothing that counted."

"This one does?"

"How about you?" Donald said. "How can you just go on alone? Don't you want something warm in your bed?"

"I seem to be managing."

Donald took a long swallow of beer.

"Why did you come to the funeral?" Arnold said.

"I don't like knowing too much," Donald said. "It's better if you don't know too much, I always thought that. But when you called and told me they found the old man's body, I got thinking about him. Couldn't stop. No matter what I did, I couldn't goddam stop, and all of a sudden, I knew what it was like for him, with Sandra, how he couldn't leave her alone."

"It took you thirty years to figure that out."

"I was a kid. He was my father. He abandoned mother. I didn't want to know. I still don't."

"Maybe now the same thing's happening to you?"

"Nothing's happening to me. I let someone get under my skin is all."

"How about Daphne?"

"Nothing about Daphne. Daphne's fine."

"She doesn't know about this other woman."

"There's nothing to know."

"Except you're thinking of jumping off roofs."

"Nothing to do with it."

"You certainly do think it's better not to know too much."

"Why aren't you going crazy with loneliness, Arnold? I'd like to know that."

"I'm lonely sometimes."

"But you don't do anything about it."

"I'm a bit of a hermit in ways."

They drank and sat still, surrounded by the noise and activity, as if they were on a raft in the middle of a billowing ocean.

"Mother was beautiful, wasn't she?" Donald said. "When she was young?"

"I think so. She looks beautiful in the photographs."

"And she was special?"

"She was clever, and difficult. Yes, she was special."

"She died so young."

"She wasn't strong."

"I hated it all so much, the old man and Sandra, and then you running after Sandra with your tongue hanging out."

"Was it so obvious?"

"You were in love with her. She wasn't that much older than you, and she couldn't stop flirting with you."

"I think she needed to feel somebody in the family accepted her."

"Are you still in love with her?"

"No."

"You wouldn't tell me the truth if you were."

"When father first disappeared, and I came out here, Sandra told me something strange. That he'd been talking more and more about mother, obsessively almost. Sandra thought he'd killed himself in some irrational attempt to get to where mother was."

Donald was staring at him, his eyes wide, a little crazed. Arnold wondered if telling him had been a terrible mistake, but he met his brother's look and held it.

"Poor bitch," Donald said, at last, and reached for his glass.

"Sandra?"

"When you think about it," Donald said, "women don't get much of a break, do they? They don't get much of a break."

"I'd never thought of it that way."

"Daphne's tough," Donald said. "I always liked that about her. She's tough. She takes no shit."

He got up from the table.

"I'm going to my room," he said. "You coming?"

"I think I'll finish my drink."

Donald nodded and walked away, his legs pushing the burly body ahead of them as if he was walking through water up to his chest, upriver, against a powerful current. He vanished through the doorway.

She had been in bed for three days, one of those moods or depressions or spells of unexplained sickness that overtook her from time to time. In the morning, Arnold would bring her tea and a plate of arrowroot biscuits, and during the day, she would nibble at them. Though she had the lights out and the window blinds drawn, he would find her, when he came home from school, with a book in her hand, held close to her face, her thin shoulders hunched, her tiny hands gripping the edges of the book as if it might fly away unless she held to it very hard. The skin over her nose would be tight and shiny, the pupils of her eyes enlarged until they looked like the eyes of some timorous nocturnal creature, and these lost, diffident, swollen eyes were hidden far back in the bones of the skull, shaded by the eyebrows that grew surprisingly thick on that slender transparent face. At dinnertime, most days, Arnold would make soup and take a bowl of it to his mother, who would lift the spoon to her mouth with quick repeated gestures, like the gestures of oriental men eating with chopsticks, which he had seen when his father had taken him and Donald for dinner in Chinatown. After two or three days of this, the spell would lift and she would resume her role as mother, arranging things, running the household.

Today he had made chicken noodle soup and put it in three bowls on the table, then sent Donald up with one for their mother, on a wooden tray. When Donald didn't return, Arnold put his soup back in the pan on a low heat. Donald would stay with her now until she had finished her soup and perhaps afterward, talking. Arnold sipped his own bowl of soup, pursuing the slippery noodles so that they weren't all left in a soggy mess at the bottom. He ate some crackers and a bit of cheese, but didn't bother making anything else. Later he'd go over to Yonge Street for a club sandwich.

When he went out at night, he always had an excuse—that he was hungry and needed a sandwich or he wanted to drop a book in the slot at the library, though he knew that the apparent reasons were only the thinnest of pretexts. He went because he was compelled. He had abandoned his old, childish phrase, no longer thought of himself as Master of the Night City, but he still needed the reassurance it gave him to travel through the city alone, to observe. Sometimes he went downtown, by the Brown Derby, and watched the night people, the sharp-looking ones and the sleazy pathetic ones, their eyes dimmed and brains blown out by alcohol and drugs. One night he had seen two women fighting, their high voices sharp as knives. One tore clothing from the other, and Arnold had seen a thin pathetic breast, and the woman had noticed him watching and turned and spat. "No free shows," she shouted.

Other nights, he walked down the back lanes, looking in windows, not stopping, for he was afraid of being discovered and arrested. In front of one window, he might see a man and woman kissing, through another, a solitary figure tidying. Once he had seen a man beating a woman with slow, patient, determined blows of his fist. It surprised him how many people left blinds and curtains open. Every single house was full of lives; there was a frightening multiplicity. He'd thought that one night as he walked down a back lane west of the university. They should call the city the multiplicity, he thought, and when he got home, he wrote it down in a notebook he kept.

Donald appeared at the kitchen door carrying the tray and the empty soup bowl.

"She's worse than usual," he said.

"I don't think so. She was reading this afternoon."

"It's because he came."

A few days before, their father had visited the house to see her. He was about to leave town for a week, and there was some kind of business he had to sort out.

"He should stay away from her," Donald said. "She's always worse when she sees him."

"There's business they have to discuss."

"He comes because he wants to see her. Sandra's only good for one thing, and when he gets tired of that, he comes to see mother."

"Did she eat the soup?" Arnold said.

"Yeah."

"Did you ask her if she wanted anything else?"

"I'm going to make her a piece of toast."

"You better have something to eat too."

"Don't give me orders."

"You have to eat."

"What have you had?"

"Some crackers and cheese. I'm going to go out later and get a sandwich."

"Can I come?"

"No."

"Why?"

"I'm meeting somebody."

"A girl?"

"Maybe."

"Does she put out?"

"None of your business."

Donald went to the breadbox and took out a loaf of sliced cracked-wheat bread.

"You should make yourself a sandwich," Arnold said.

"Jesus, why won't you shut up?"

"All right."

"Just go out and get your ashes hauled up some dark alley. Give her a poke for me."

Arnold had no plan to meet anyone, but he knew it was the simplest way to get away on his own. Often he and his brother went out together in the evening,

bowling or to a show, a western if Donald had anything to do with it, and sat around a restaurant
afterwards, but tonight he had to be on his own. He
wanted the sense of danger and secrecy. He would
have preferred not even to have admitted he was
going. It was like masturbating; he didn't like to know
he was planning it in advance; it was better if it just
happened. He was aware that his mind was duplici-
tous, that he did know in advance about both these
private activities, even though he did not let himself
admit his plans. He would always pretend that something different might happen.

There was another plan that he was not letting
himself know.

"Anything good on television tonight?" Arnold
said.

"Not much."

"I might come and watch for a while."

Their father had bought them a television set a few
months before, in time for the World Series. They
were the first people in the neighbourhood to have
one, but their mother disapproved of it and refused to
allow it in the living-room, so the set was kept in
Donald's room, since he watched it the most. He
sometimes complained when Arnold came in to
watch, but the complaints weren't meant with any
seriousness. He liked having company. Sometimes the
two of them would watch together until after mid-
night. Once or twice their mother, wandering the
house in her dressing-gown, had found them there,
and in spite of herself joined them in front of the blue,
blinking screen. She criticized everything she saw and
grumbled about the time they were wasting, and all
three of them enjoyed it enormously.

Arnold went to his room and sat down at his desk

to do some homework. Outside the window he could see the lights of the Jesperson's front porch, the head-lights of a car passing from time to time. These things tempted him out into the night, but he turned his eyes away and tried to concentrate on his French exercise. He took a pen. He wrote. But outside in the teeming darkness of the night, the naked daring possibilities called to him.

He worked, waited. Soon he would go and see his mother, ask her if there was anything she needed, perhaps sit on the edge of the bed and talk for a few minutes. When he was out, at night, wandering the streets and lanes, he always hoped that his mother was asleep, vanished into whatever complex and ter-rible dreams gripped her.

Once or twice he had wakened in bed at night, aware that he was being watched, he had seen his mother's thin figure wrapped in her pale-blue dress-ing-gown, a shadow by the door of the room.

"Go back to bed, mother," he said once when he saw her there, and she nodded.

"I know," she said. "I know you're fine. You're a fine boy. Sometimes I just have to see you, to know that you're real."

The figure vanished, silently, as if it might have been something he dreamed.

Another night, he woke and saw the dark shape among the shapes of the room.

"Yes, mother," he said, in a voice that was dragged out of the heavy ways of sleep, "I'm real."

"No," she said. "Not real enough, Arnold. Not real enough to save me."

And he fell back asleep, or she walked away, he couldn't tell which.

Je les avais vus, he wrote, remembering to make the past participle agree with the preceding direct object. *Je les avais vus. I have seen them.* Who? The men and women behind the windows, buttering bread, talking to someone who was hidden in another part of the room. *Je les avais vus.* Once he had seen a woman, her back to him, held in the embrace of some man, who had his hands under her lifted skirt, inside her underpants, caressing, exploring. Then they moved away from the window and turned off the light, and Arnold stood in the dark lane, his heart beating fast, his legs trembling a little, his body heated with excitement and an edge of terror. He remembered the way the woman's body squirmed against the man as his hand went inside her clothes.

Arnold began to run down the lane, and didn't stop running until he was out of breath.

Je les avais vus.

Elle est venue chez mois. Conjugated with *être,* the past participle agreed with the subject. *Je suis venu chez elle.* The thought took on form, but he put it away. He wouldn't know. Not yet.

Arnold finished the exercise and put his books in a pile on the edge of the desk, then went down the hall and stood listening outside the door of his mother's room, wondering if he could tell by her breathing whether or not she was awake.

"Arnold. Come in."

"I thought you might be asleep," he said, as he opened the door.

A book lay on the bed beside her, a collection of short stories by John O'Hara.

"Is that a good book?"

"He's very cynical, isn't he?"

"I don't know. I haven't read anything by him."

"I think he's a hard-hearted man. I think he might be cruel. If you knew him."

The eyes were bright, as if the secret creature who dwelt within them had suddenly lighted on something astonishing.

"Do you think you can really tell what an author's like from his stories?" Arnold said.

"They always let on something they don't mean to. Like someone you meet who's trying so hard to make an impression, but you can tell that they're shy or silly or thoughtless underneath it all."

Her small fingers began to massage her forehead.

"Is your head aching?"

"A little."

"Do you want an aspirin? Or shall I make some tea?"

"No. I'm all right. I think I'm a little better today."

Arnold knew from past experience that tomorrow, or a day or two later, he and Donald would get up in the morning to find their mother already at work in the kitchen, breakfast on the table, tea biscuits hot from the oven, the dishes that had piled up all washed and put away. For a day or so she would be gay, then simply quiet and distant, and again, sooner or later, she would begin to look tired and strained, the bright eyes would sink into the skull and she would take to her bed.

They chatted for a few minutes more, and when he was leaving, Arnold told her the same version of the truth that he had told Donald, that he was meeting a friend and going over to Yonge Street. His mother, as if she recognized and respected the lie, did not ask him who the friend might be.

Outside it was all different. He was someone new,

free. Quickly he walked through the quiet Rosedale streets, taking the route that led him north and then west to Yonge. He looked at the busy traffic going north and south, excited by the sense of activity, men and women on errands of business or pleasure.

When he'd sat down in the restaurant where he was something of a regular and ordered his club sandwich, he leaned back in the corner of the booth, to watch the proprietor, who at this time of night was both waiter and cook, put the sandwich together. For the first time, Arnold admitted to himself that he was going to his father's house. To spy on Sandra. Or perhaps go boldly to the door and knock.

Could he pretend that he didn't know his father was out of town? No. It was better not to lie. I just dropped in for a visit, he'd say. I thought you might be lonely. Perhaps he shouldn't say that. I thought you might like a visitor.

What did she do when his father was out of town? Arnold couldn't quite imagine. Maybe she had a lot of friends who came to see her. What if she was with a man?

He remembered her, last summer on the dock at the cottage, trying to wrestle him into the water. He remembered how she looked. Exactly. The female shape, the texture of the skin and hair. How, as he and Donald were leaving, when for a moment she and Arnold had been left alone, she had kissed him on the cheek, and whispered her thanks. Thank you for liking me, she said, and the warmth of her lips was against his skin.

Arnold didn't understand why Donald disliked her so much. She was beautiful and warm, generous. She wouldn't be too shocked if he knocked on her door. She knew the world. Knew, he felt sure, that he couldn't stop looking at her last summer when she wore shorts or a bathing suit. Her tanned skin was a soft amber, and he was sure that if he touched it, it would be silken. He knew, from that moment on the dock, the exact colour of her secret hair.

When the club sandwich, thick and dripping with mayonnaise, was on the table in front of him, Arnold was not sure he wanted it any longer. His mind was already further on into the night, watching Sandra's house, going inside it to see her. But he began to eat the sandwich, and as he ate, discovered that he was, after all, hungry, and quickly it was finished.

Back on the street, he turned north. His father's new house was north of St Clair, not far from Upper Canada College. Once his mother had suggested that he and Donald should attend UCC, but his father had defended them in their desire to stay in the public schools. His father had grown up in a small town, and though he was at home with the men who sent their sons to UCC, he had a loyalty to his country roots that made him uncomfortable with the thought of his sons going there.

His father might be in the house with Sandra, returned early from his trip. If Arnold crept up to the window and looked in, he might see the two of them involved in one of Donald's more vivid fantasies. Arnold tried to remember if he had ever seen his father naked. He thought not. The man was very reticent. Could he be so with Sandra? If so, why had he left his wife for her? Though Arnold refused to participate in Donald's crude inventions about the couple, he assumed that they were, in essence, true, that the thing between them was baldly sexual and that was, perhaps, part of the reason that he was walking toward the house. What would she be like left on her own? There was a need to see her, to understand what she might be like. To look at her from close up. And he enjoyed her company. They were always easy together, able to talk about inconsequential things. Sandra was not, like his mother, an inveterate reader, but she encouraged Arnold to talk to her about books, and she listened in a way that was interested and yet detached. She didn't make it seem too important the way his mother did, hungry to hear his thoughts and declare her own. Sandra was easier to talk with. Arnold found that when he was close to her, he was tempted to reach out and touch her, in a friendly way, as if he knew she'd be pleased.

He was walking quickly, and soon he was off Yonge and on one of the quiet residential streets that would take him to the house he was seeking. The lights were on in the large, expensively decorated living-room of one of the houses he passed, but the room was empty. Waiting. Waiting for someone to enter, the scene to begin.

When he was close to the house, he began to walk more slowly. He approached it on the far side of the street, his heart making him aware of its hard beating. There weren't many lights on, and Arnold wondered if Sandra might have gone out. The thought was both a relief and a disappointment. The porch light was on, and a dim light behind the wide window at the front. The stained-glass window beside the stairs was almost dark, though there was one upstairs light on, toward the back. For a moment Arnold stood still on the pavement and stared, as if he might develop mystic powers of vision and see through the walls. It was a cool September night, and as he stood there, he saw a couple of leaves fall from a tree nearby. He could hear traffic in the distance and feel a little wind.

The house was silent. Slowly he crossed the street, always with the sense that someone was observing him. There was no one visible nearby, but he knew he could be seen from a dozen windows. As quietly as he could, he walked down the little alley beside the house, into the backyard. The shade on the dining-room window was drawn, but there was an inch or two uncovered at the bottom. Arnold placed one foot carefully after the other as he walked across the lawn to the window. It was a little above eye level. He wondered if he could find something to stand on, but that was too dangerous, too crazy. When he had come here before, he had always stayed at a distance, across the street, or on the neighbour's driveway. Slowly, he backed away from the window, until he was at an angle where he could see a narrow slice of the room. Most of his view was blocked by the dining-room table and chairs, but at one side, part of the living-room was visible, and there, emerging from the hall doorway, was Sandra, just her neck and torso; blue tailored slacks and a white blouse. She passed across the room and disappeared and Arnold was chilled and trembling, convinced that she knew he was here. Quickly, but as quietly as he could, he walked down the alley to the street and away and for the next hour, he walked frantically, at random, through the night streets, trying to move fast enough to stop himself thinking. There was nothing remarkable in what he had seen, Sandra's neatly dressed shape moving across the room and vanishing, but the memory excited and disturbed him. It was possible now to go home, go to bed, consider the whole thing an abortive adventure, but it would be an act of cowardice. The thought of going back terrified him, but he had to go.

He was at the door, ringing the bell. When she

opened it, he would be unable to speak. He would babble foolishly.

"Arnold."

"I thought you might like some company."

"Come in. I was just wishing somebody would call or drop in."

As Arnold walked past her, he was aware of a smell of liquor on her breath, and he was startled that she would be drinking alone. He thought of that as something that tragically unhappy people did, sitting by themselves at night, drinking.

"Sit down," Sandra said. A radio or record player was on quietly somewhere in the background, playing slow dance music. On the floor by one of the chairs was a silver cocktail shaker.

"I just made a martini. Would you like one?"

"Sure."

"I'll get a glass."

She went to the sideboard in the dining-room. Behind her was the window with the small uncovered section below the blind where he had peered in and seen her moving past to her chair.

She came back with the glass and poured him a drink, and when she gave it to him, there was no suggestion—as there usually was when adults offered him drinks—that this was something illegal, something special. She just handed him the drink, and he put it to his lips, a little repulsed by the bitter perfumy taste and smell. He sipped it and felt as if the effect on his brain was immediate. Everything in the room was a little luminous, a little odd. It was something he'd be unable to describe, he thought, in one of his notebooks, something real, but too subtle for words.

Sandra was leaning back in her chair, her legs stretched out in front of her, crossed at the ankles.

"What do you do with yourself, Arnold? Apart from school."

"There's quite a bit to do at the house. The lawns and gardens in the summer, snow and coal and ashes in the winter. Sometimes Donald and I go bowling. Sometimes I just walk around the city."

It felt dangerous, saying that, as if he might be coming close to telling her the truth about his haunted nights. Was she someone he could tell? He sipped the drink. The taste was a little nauseating. Sandra was looking at him, and he felt his legs shaking as he looked back, memorized the shape and position of her body.

"Do you go dancing?"

"Sometimes I go to dances at the school."

"When I was your age, I used to love to go dancing. On Saturday nights, sometimes, I'd go down to the Palais Pier with some of my friends, and the place was always full of soldiers in uniform. The war was still on then, and we'd dance and dance with all those handsome soldiers and sailors and airmen."

Arnold took another swallow of his drink. He was getting used to the taste now.

"I remember one night," she said, "when I was dancing with this thin boy with a sweet face and lovely long eyelashes, like yours, and he said that he was going overseas, and he promised that if I danced with him all evening, he'd send me postcards from everywhere he went. I got one, from London, but then I never heard from him again. I was seventeen, and he wasn't much older."

"I suppose if the war was still on, I'd be in the army," Arnold said.

"You'd look handsome in a uniform. Air Force. That would suit your colouring."

Arnold had never heard Sandra talk in quite this way. She must be a little drunk. The lines of her face were softened, even more beautiful, and yet there was something a little blurred, a little dangerous about her. His hands couldn't be still for wanting her. Some terrible decision hung in the air, and the presence of someone watching him. Something in him that wanted to scream. Words of love or dire obscenities. He couldn't quite tell which.

The record player—or radio, whichever it was—was playing "Deep Purple".

"I haven't danced for a long time," Sandra said.

She was looking at him.

"Would you like to dance?" she said.

Arnold stood up and walked toward her and reached out his hand. She took it in her own warm hand and stood up, moving into his arms with a grace and ease that he'd never known with the girls he piloted around the floor of the school auditorium. He felt the touch of her breasts.

"It's not easy to dance on the rug," he said.

"We're doing OK."

Their bodies slid sweetly against each other to the sound of the music until Arnold's excitement was almost too much for him. He wanted to hold her even closer, to reach beneath her clothes to her smooth skin. His eyes kept noticing details of the room, the little slice of window revealed beneath the dining-room window shade. A man stood out there in the cold spying on them.

The song came to an end, and he looked at Sandra's face, the brightness that seemed to come from somewhere within the blue, intent eyes, that examined him, held him; he smelled the winy sharpness of her breath, and then they were kissing, hot and open-mouthed, her body against his, fluid and accepting. He was swollen and trembling and pressed harder against her until he caught his breath and the semen poured out of him. He could feel the wetness in his underwear, his trousers, down his leg, wet, sticky and hot, and he was ashamed, and drew back and saw her face, the face of his father's wife, slack and ardent.

The wet patch was soaking through his trousers. He didn't want her to see it, this childishness, and he was chilled and frightened by what they had done. He held her away from him.

"I have to go," he said, and turned his back so that she wouldn't see. He tried to walk normally to the door of the room.

"Arnold."

He turned only his head, kept his shame covered. Now she looked worried, defeated.

"You won't ever tell anyone, will you?" she said. There was a dreadful importuning sound to the words, the despair of one who has lost all dignity.

"No," he said, not turning, hiding the wet, stained clothing, "I won't. Not ever."

Arnold lay on his back in the strange bed, staring up at a line of light from the motel window, listening to the sound of a car driving away from the parking lot outside. He had stayed too long alone in the noisy bar, drunk too much whisky, and he felt a little as if, when he closed his eyes, he might be dizzy and confused.

He wondered who the woman was who had invaded his brother's life; he tried to imagine what she might be like, and of course there was no way of knowing. Desire was unpredictable, inexplicable. Lust, like charity, was generic, all women and all men were the same in the dark, whether the dark of animal need or the dark of lost humans seeking kindness. But *eros* (bad god, bad god) was a particular madness, not to be understood except as the arbitrary infliction of a malevolent minor deity, vivid and dangerous and not to be sated ever, quite, by any paroxysm of flesh and nerves, for it took aim at the separateness, the uniqueness of the fiery individual soul. Were some individuals especially dangerous, lightning rods who drew the fire from the sky because they were deeply grounded in the earth or below, because they drew sparks to the negative charge of their dark needs? That Sandra had captured his father's soul, and (to admit the truth) for a while his own, was a mystery. She was no more beautiful than many other women, no more intelligent. She had always been quiet, restrained. Perhaps it was those whose need for love was a reticent starvation who drew others most dangerously to destruction. The sirens, male and female. Who gave back, at last, nothing; the Lorelei is only an echoing rock.

Today his father's already half-rotted body, recovered from the ocean, had been placed in a hole in the earth, and in the house she had shared with him, Sandra lay alone, growing older. The whisky told him that there was some important conclusion to be drawn, but he could not capture it.

Arnold would fall asleep and wake in the night, not knowing where he was.

9

It gleamed, lustrous, almost iridescent, a sheen like dark water. Julia sat and studied the swatch of fine hair, in part only admiring, in part trying to analyze the colours that composed this brown so dark it was almost black, and yet, in light, seen to be riddled with other tints.

The hair was held together with elastics, cut bluntly at one end where the scissors had severed it, but at the other, fine, slightly uneven lengths. Elena had been about to have the ends trimmed when Julia asked her if she could have it.

She had cut it with large, very sharp scissors so that she could take off the swatch all at once, with a single cut. Then, when she had gathered it safely into the elastics, she went back to where Elena sat and trimmed the remaining hair into a kind of shag that revealed the delicate shape of the skull, and when that was done and Elena had dared to look in a mirror,

Julia put away the chunk of hair in a wooden box she had found in a junk store, a long wooden box covered with rosewood veneer, the red and black of the rosewood a chromatic inversion of the black penetrated by cinnamon lustres of the hair.

This was to be the hair of Lilith, who would be queen of one segment of her puppet world, the queen of the ancient times; around her, like stars, a gathering of the names she had been called, the screech owl, the night lily, temptress, cannibal of children, and to one side of her, the figures of Adam and Eve, Eve bald, with the glass eyes of a doll, Adam hanging inverted as a limp penis suspended from a transparent plastic male torso with ancient stories painted on it.

What if the Adam puppet had been there, completed, when she had arrived back, Jimmy, the bartender's friend, leaping out of the car to open the door for her, a pat on the shoulder for reassurance, Yes Jimmy, I'm fine, and if the penis puppet had hung there, she would have taken her utility knife and sliced it off.

She tried to imagine the puppets in place, the whole world assembled. It would take forever to finish her project, and maybe it could only be completed within the environment where it would be permanently installed. She needed three-dimensional spaces, lighting, a way for the viewer to move from one perspective to another. Perhaps the male torso should be the crucified figure of Jesus and the stories should only be visible from behind, the front of the torso flesh-coloured, but with no back so that within, when viewed from behind, one could see a retelling of other Biblical stories, in a style that was a blend of medieval art and the comic book narrative, stories from Greece and Rome and Palestine, all visible at the same time.

How was she to find a place for it all?

She could assemble sections of the whole panorama on wheeled wagons, small enough to be taken out the old garage doors. When one or two of them were done, she could show them and hope that some institution would offer her a room for the whole installation. Not that it seemed likely. Institutions were run by men, or if by women, by tamed or careful or ambitious women. Judy Chicago had found museums to show "The Dinner Party," but it was less vehement, less rough-edged than what Julia was planning. She was mortally engaged in the creation of a work that had no hope of a permanent home, no hope of completion. But that was suitable for this woman's history of the world. It would be wrong to create a monument.

It took almost too much faith to work, these days, the world poisoned, the missiles poised, bad old men everywhere raping the universe. In her last year at art school, she had done a series of cartoon paintings about the dire old men who were threatening to destroy the planet. The show had somehow got reviewed in the *Star* and the man who did it called the paintings shrill. Julia took that as a compliment.

On the way out of the bar, Jimmy trying to take her arm—stupid gallantry—there was a young woman, standing by the door, all white and raspberry, her hair bleached and fluffed, raspberry socks over white ribbed tights and a long raspberry sweater, pulled very snug over the hips and ending just below— advertising herself, putting herself up for sale.

Lilith must embody the female rejection of servitude to the violent world. Imagine Abraham prepared to sacrifice Isaac, and Sarah left behind somewhere in the tent to wait for the news of the event to be brought by her master. Obey me, Adam said, and Lilith responded, No, we are equal, made of the same earth.

Her body must suggest the colour of earth, the weight of earth, heavy and powerful. Naked or clothed? To suggest her power, she should be naked, but there might be something objectified, something potentially pornographic about that. Maybe there ought to be a number of Liliths, all combined, aspects of the same woman goddess. She might be portrayed naked, giving birth, and the child half-revealed between her thighs is a miniature version of herself, the same dark long shining hair.

And how to incorporate the dirty stories told about Lilith, the evil gossip spread about her because she has had the courage to assert herself? A sign labelled *Gossip*? Or a TV screen with a picture of Lilith and a tape of all the gossip playing, a little overspeed so that the voice is distorted and anyone who hears it can recognize the untruth of the old tale. *Lilith eats her children, Lilith eats her children, Lilith eats her children.*

She would not be a multiple figure, but only a triple one, the naked mother giving birth to the child who is her new avatar, and above, standing on her own swollen naked belly, a Lilith in queenly robes, splendid in self-assertion. Nearby, Eve, wimpish, bald, shaven, powerless, the obedient schoolgirl.

She took up a piece of paper and began to sketch the shapes, and wondered, as she did, whether she had enough hair for the three figures, the Lilith who gave birth, the regal figure above, and the half-born child. Could she go to Elena for more? It would take years to grow enough, but it must be the same hair. It was the colours that were magic, the iridescent darkness, and that it was Elena's hair and given to her voluntarily, that she had cut it with her own hands, that it was a link between the two of them.

The TV screen. It was a good idea, though perhaps it didn't need to be an operating set, only the front screen painted with a likeness of Lilith, in a dot format, a pointillist portrait, with letters across the bottom: Female Criminal Lilith, and from inside the set, the distorted voice: *Lilith eats her children, Lilith eats her children, Lilith eats her children.*

Julia took another sheet of paper and began to sketch the whole segment of the installation, the torso of the male god with its pendant Adam, dim Eve, the triple Lilith, perhaps some kind of nuclear war between God and Satan in the air above. Sarah. Sarah and Jehovah and Abraham and Isaac. The story is Sarah's nightmare, her worst dream, that the man, impelled by his loyalty to the barbaric father god, has taken a knife to kill her son. It must be seen on her face, that this is the price of obedience. The face should be made of plaster of Paris, very lightly painted, with a sense of the hardness, the stoniness of the plaster, that Sarah has been turned to stone by the vision of bloodletting that she has seen. Or she is only a face appearing out of the stone at the scene of the sacrifice. As Abraham raises the knife, she is the sorrowing observer, her face a part of the cliff. As Lilith is made of earth so is Sarah, but earth which has gone hard with the fear of what she has seen.

On her work table a Gideon Bible lay open at the passage which, she had read somewhere, was a reference to Lilith, night demon, screech owl.

The satyr shall cry to his fellow; the screech owl also shall rest there, and find for herself a place of rest.

Visions of a mad old man. The Book of Hate.

She tossed away her pencil, took a piece of charcoal and turning it on its side began to cover the paper with wide black strokes, plumage, feathered breasts, wide eyes, a screaming mouth, Lilith as prophetess, answering back to these old men.

As a child, raised free, godless, she had never read the Bible, only heard it now and then in school, but when she was in art school, a friend had convinced her that she ought to know something about it, and had stolen this Gideon Bible from a motel where she worked summers as a chambermaid. Late at night the two of them would get it out and read it aloud to each other, laughing and gasping over the craziness of it all.

On a second sheet, she was forming another of the black owl-women, and when it was done, she was spent, threw down the drawing, took a can of fixative and sprayed the drawing, then went and fell on the bed, her hands, still covered with black charcoal, covering her face, rubbing against the skin, dirtying herself. Before long it would be time for work. Going to Elena's to change, she would walk through the streets like this, blackened, stained with charcoal. Like a chimney sweep.

She rubbed the dust into her skin. It had sunk into her deeper than she thought, the attack the night before. A customer, very drunk, had cornered her in the narrow hall coming back from the toilet. All night he had been overtipping her, and she had taken the money and attempted to ignore the crude patter that went with it. He was a pale man, with straight grey hair and false teeth that were a little too big and bright. He had watched her go down the dark hallway toward the toilet, and when she came out he was waiting for her.

"Feel better now?" he said.

Julia didn't answer, just tried to make her way past him.

"Sure you wiped it dry? Don't want a pissy pussy," he said and reached for her. Once again she tried to get past him, but now he pushed her against the wall, and stuck a hand between her legs, began groping her with hard fingers, squeezing and probing, his other hand on one of her breasts as she struggled to push him off. The bar was full of customers and she couldn't quite bring herself to shout, but neither could she push him off, and she was at the point of crying out when she felt the man torn away from her, and saw Manuel, the Portuguese bartender, a long knife in his hand, pinning the man against the far wall.

"You get out," Manuel was saying. "You get out and you don't come back. You come back and I cut your balls off." The knife was very close to the man's body, and Manuel, his face pale and empty, looked absolutely prepared to use it. He dragged the man toward the back door. As they moved away, Julia fled into the washroom and locked herself in one of the cubicles.

Not to cry, that was the first thing, and she stood breathing slowly and deeply and drove the tears back, tightened her jaws, the muscles of her face, made everything still, breathed more slowly, closed her eyes and confronted the face of the man coming down over hers. He had tried to kiss her. She bent and threw up into the toilet, and gasped as if to set loose sobs, but held them in. If the tears started, there would be no end to them. She stood and straightened her uniform, unlocked the cubicle and went to the sink where she splashed water on her face.

When she went out, she would have to confront Manuel. She had never much liked him. His attitude to her, to all women, was rigid, old-fashioned, half-barbaric. Women should stay at home and make babies. But he was, within his own medieval standards, at least honourable, and there had been a glittering second of relief when she had found him with her, on her side, armed. She had not known that he carried a knife or kept one behind the bar; if she were to think carefully about Manuel, she would probably reckon him a dangerous man. He was a man who could kill, the sort whose moral standards were primitive and absolute, savage. She was opposed to what he stood for, but she was grateful to have had him on her side. Impossible; it was all, always impossible, to deal with men and their world.

She dried her face and went into the hall and down toward the bar.

As she reached the bar, Manuel looked her over as if he might be checking her for signs of damage, and then held out a tumbler with a large shot of rum in it.

"You drink that down, then I get Jimmy to drive you home."

"I'm OK," Julia said.

Jimmy was Manuel's pal, a union carpenter who came in every night and sat at the far end of the bar. He was looking toward them from his seat, his eyes heavy, protective, hateful.

"I'm OK," Julia said. "I'll finish my shift."

"Don't give me horseshit, Julia. You drink that and go with Jimmy."

Julia didn't have the strength to fight back. She knew if she argued with him, she'd start to cry, but she hated this, letting him look after her. It wasn't worth a scene, and OK, he meant well. She drank the rum and cashed out.

Now as she lay on the bed, rubbing charcoal into her face, she found that she was imagining the scene differently, the knife penetrating the skin, the long pale face growing grey, then greenish, yellowish in death. She could still feel the fingers between her thighs. Perhaps she should carry a knife of her own, then she wouldn't be at the mercy of Manuel or whatever other self-elected saviour passed by.

There had been an arrangement to meet her father today, for lunch, to get the news about the funeral, her grandfather's will, but she had phoned him and cancelled. She was still too much gripped by the assault, might blurt out something about it. She did not say such things to her father, never had. He was not good at hearing the truth. It was not one of his talents. It would be too dangerous to try, to start, if once Julia told him a true thing, too many others might follow, a deluge of hard truths, most particularly, the one true, unspeakable thing, that he had destroyed her mother, that he had ruined the woman's life, stifled it in lukewarm affections and a vacuous adherence to conventions. Julia remembered, dreaded to remember, that empty cheerfulness that propelled her mother through her days, a polite surface of decency that covered unknown depths of stifled horror.

After her mother's death, Julia helped to sort and send away her things, her head aching, her stomach raw with nausea, and she remembered finding the package with the diaphragm and jelly and plastic device for insertion. Her mother had periodically impaled herself on this ancient device so that her father might penetrate her. It was all, their whole life, out of the dark ages.

The first moment it seemed possible, Julia had moved out of the apartment, desperate to escape from those airless rooms, that woman drying away to dust, her colours all pale, dusty, grey, dim lavender blue, sickly pink, ivory, the way her mother allowed herself to be caught up in her father's dilettante enthusiasm for things Chinese, dutifully following him to exhibitions, stores, auctions, letting herself be surrounded by the pallor, the excessive delicacy of the things he bought. Would she have allowed her feet to be bound if that was required?

Airless, smothering rooms. Were all homes like that? Old shame, old anger hung in every cupboard like an out-of-date suit that still fitted its owner perfectly. Stale, oppressive. She could do something with that, the idea of old clothes, a photograph or an installation, families of clothing. She could tell the story of her life in old clothes, her Doctor Denton's, her little pink and white dresses, the plaid woolen lumberjack shirt which they got on an outing to Algonquin Park and which she had insisted on wearing to school, over her father's strong objection. The more he objected, the more determined she was to wear it, and did, every day, until it was in shreds. Her father thought she wore it to impress her contemporaries, but it was not that. The girls had taken it as another opportunity to mock her, but she didn't mind. She loved the shirt. It seemed to have some message for her about who she was, and even now, when she was working, she wore similar shirts, heavy, rough-textured, filthy with glue and paint and dust. They were like a kind of armour she wore so that within she could be naked enough to do her work.

What if her mother's clothes, the slightly out-of-date tweeds and cashmeres had been a kind of armour? No, there was no freedom within. They adhered to her body, dermatological symptoms of some subtle invasive disease. Within her, the cells had grown dim, dry, moribund, and she had died, and after her death, Julia had cried until her bones ached, then she staggered and fell and cried more. Finally after days of this hidden tearing of her being, Elena had caught her in the act. Until then, she had kept it hidden, this desperate, harsh grief, but Elena, who was half a stranger then, had found her, and sat beside her, talking softly, as she might to a maddened animal, until she brought her back to sense.

Without that calming voice, without that gentle touch, she thought, she would have cried herself to death. She had, until then, always assumed Elena was fragile, almost too delicate to live. But she had proved to be made of some fine-drawn, shining material of great tensile strength. Elena had insisted on being brought to the apartment that Julia had fled. She wanted to meet her father, and they had sat together over a not-very-inspired dinner that Julia had cooked during the afternoon, and they had drunk too much wine and talked. Commonplace enough, but that dinner had given Julia a certain peace, as Elena had perhaps foreseen. After two glasses of wine, she had found herself looking at her father as Elena might look at him, seeing a man not without sensitivity, not without a certain wit, even a kind of charm in his slightly laborious patrician manner. She saw him, for once, as a human being.

It had been easier since then. Different memories had returned, memories that were easier to live with. And some that were harder as well. From some closet in the back halls of the mind had come a memory of a day after the death of her grandmother. Julia, too young to have known the woman well, or even to have realized the significance of her death, had toddled into a room, and seen her father, his back turned to her, his head bent, held in his hands, and when she had spoken, he had turned suddenly, his face wet and raw, terrifying, and he had shouted and waved her away, and turned once again to be hidden from her.

She could not remember where she had gone, perhaps she had found her mother and been comforted. It had all vanished except that moment of horror, that bare, damaged face that was no longer her father.

It was a classic instance: he was not present in his marriage because he had never got free of his mother, that inadequate, clinging woman who had left both her sons scarred, and by a terrible irony of the sort that patriarchal society fostered, had, by the enduring effect of her own unhappiness, tainted the life of her son's wife. And if her grandmother was inadequate, clinging, she had been made so by a tyrannical father, unfaithful husband.

There must be an end to it, the pain of generations, the generations of pain. She would proclaim an end. She would stand up like Lilith in her puppet landscape. She would strap on a knife. Elena had made Julia consider her father as a human being, but she would not forgive him for her mother's destruction, which left her deserted and alone.

She sat on the edge of the bed, looked around the bleak bare room. She liked it. It was ugly, spacious, functional, stained with grease, and she was often happy here, alone with her work, though she never regarded the place as anything better than temporary. Although she paid rent, she always felt she was here on sufferance, that her uncle, struck by a whim, a moment of inexplicable malice, would someday arrive at the door, unexpected, as he always was, unlikely, mysteriously puzzled, half-wicked, and would send her away. Last week, when she went to the tattoo parlour with her rent—late as usual—there was a woman there, drinking coffee with him, a skinny blonde in shorts and a tank top—something intimate between them. The woman had watched Julia with the cool eyes of a woman who was in possession of a man, a place. Maybe Julia could blackmail her uncle into letting her stay here. He was frightened of Daphne; he wouldn't want her to know what she had seen and sensed. Still, for now it was hers. The two big portraits of Elena in black and white stared down at her.

On the streets outside, the man who had attacked her in the bar was following another woman into an alley.

Behind his bar, Manuel was wiping glasses, setting the bottles of mix, the lemons, limes, olives, in order, replacing his knife in its position ready for another emergency.

Beside her bed, on a crude table she had nailed together from bits of scrap lumber, was a picture of her mother, her father, herself as a girl of twelve. She hated the picture, but all the same she kept it there beside the bed. It was the only picture she had ever seen in which her mother was laughing, and the laughter that shaped her face so beautifully offered a glimpse of another world in which she might have been happy, in which she would not have left Julia alone.

Though the most painful thing of all was the attempts she made: at Christmas, she would arrange for the two of them to spend week-ends together, baking from old family recipes. Or she would insist that the two of them should go shopping together, to refurbish Julia's wardrobe. She used that word, refurbish. Julia wanting to scream at her, Lies, Lies, Lies, I don't know who you are, I don't know who that man is that you have chosen to serve, I don't know why all your colours are pale, and your skin is dry, dusty.

But in the photograph, her mother is laughing, and her father looks a little startled, not quite composed at this momentary intervention of the comic gods into his careful world, and Julia sulking, missing the boat, too angry to catch this joyful moment. That was the most terrible possibility, that there had been happiness there, and that Julia had failed to see it.

If, when her mother had invited her to help bake for Christmas, she had been able to attend, with her whole being, would she have found that the two of them could laugh and throw flour and hug each other? No, for they both knew that if they did, Arnold might appear in the doorway, puzzled, bemused, mocking, disapproving. That still, pale, oval, even, blonde face. He would not speak, only look and go away, and at night the woman would impale herself on a device of steel and rubber, greased, and he would jiggle about on her and gasp.

Julia got up from the bed and walked back to her work table. She studied the owl-women, and now, only a few minutes after she had drawn them, they were foreign, unrecognizable, as if some other hand had made them. Yet the evidence of their creation was on her fingers, on her face. Those eyes, avian, cold, and yet with a deeper thought behind them. *Lilith eats her children.* Bites, they would say, the tight little balls off the infant boys. Sees too much, sees the dark dreams of Jehovah and must rebel.

Softness of those feathered breasts. The touch of the succubus. The bad mana of the earth shouting defiance to the sky-father. Julia was afraid of what she saw. Her own drawing made her shake.

The light on the dirty windows was growing dim as

the shadow of a tree was cast over them. It was time
to go to Elena's and get herself ready for work.
Stained, blackened, she would walk through the
streets, then showered and dressed in her waitress
uniform, she would reappear, almost respectable, a
young woman prepared to serve the needs of those
with time and money.

Before leaving, she surveyed the rags and tatters of
her puppets. What if she lost her nerve? What if she
lost her insane ability to believe in her puppet world?
Right now, at this minute, it seemed she might. The
world she had imagined would never come to be, and
she would be forever a waitress, groped in dark corners, and learning, with time, to tolerate it.

Julia took the rosewood box in her hands, opened
it, and lifting the hair by the elastics, held its softness
against her face. Love would save her. Elena would
save her.

She would run to her through the streets. She
would be held and saved.

10

The rainy light of the April afternoon drifted down through the skylights and settled on the Ming tomb. The old stone was untouched by it. It held the darkness of centuries. The stone camels stared with aristocratic hauteur at the spectacle of mortality. On the south wall, behind glass, the tomb figures were orderly assembled, a long line, motionless, immortal, a stone parade to accompany the corpse and make his claims in the world on the other side of death. Outside, on Bloor Street, behind glass, the living walked hunched under their umbrellas, waved for cabs, or ran for the shelter of buildings.

As he came into the inner gallery, Arnold saw the figure of a young woman on a camp stool beside the glass case, sketching one of the horses. Her hair was straight, and very dark, and he thought she must be Chinese, but as he walked past, he saw that her face was not oriental. There was something very still about it, and beautiful. *La chinoise*, he thought to himself, senselessly, *la chinoise*. Then he realized that he had met her before.

The horses have short legs and round, powerful bodies. They are glazed a rich brown or a pale beige with a jade-green saddle. The thick muscular necks curve upward and bend suddenly into down-turned heads with wide wild eyes, big nostrils, open mouths.

One Saturday afternoon he came here when Marie was in hospital. He had spent the morning with her and then gone back to the apartment, but once there he found himself shivering, and nothing would warm him. He tried hot coffee, heavy sweaters, but he could not stop the shaking that began somewhere deep in the marrow of his bones. He left the apartment and walked to the museum, and it was only when he was there, alone in a silent gallery, that he knew why he was so cold. He knew that Marie was going to die. He stood in front of one of the huge wall paintings sent from China by Bishop White, and he stared at the figure of Buddha who said that all suffering was caused by desire.

"It took me a minute or so to remember where I'd met you."
"I could tell."
"You recognized me."
"Yes, but I had an advantage. Julia has a picture of your family on a table in her studio."
"You did indeed have an advantage."
"She once said you took her to the museum every Sunday when she was a little girl."
"Yes."

"I envy her. My family took me to church. Presbyterian."

"We were never church goers. I suppose the museum was some kind of substitute. Something bigger than we are, something large and rare. The eternity of artifacts."

Arnold looked around the familiar room. Harold stood by the bar in his red jacket, watching for anyone who might need service. Across the room, Ray was talking to a man and woman at one of the other tables. Outside the window, the sky was grey, and the air was dark and heavy with rain. The cars on Avenue Road were starting to turn on their lights.

"Would you have dinner with me?" Arnold said.

"If you'll go to McDonald's."

"McDonald's?"

"I want to do something silly. Like taking you to McDonald's."

"Why me?"

"Because you don't belong there."

"All right."

The air over the city was darkening and yet strangely clear, luminous. The roofs, the streets, the movement of a woman crossing a road; in this light, they all had an intensity, an urgency. Because of the rain, no doubt, because of the hour, between day and night.

"Do you want another drink?" he said.

"Yes. Why not?"

Arnold signalled to Ray, who went off toward the bar to bring two more drinks.

"After Julia brought me to your apartment for dinner, there were all kinds of things I wanted to ask you."

"Then ask."

"Why the interest in Chinese art?"

"It started out with Chinese poetry. In translation — I don't know any Chinese. Amy Lowell got me started. I was interested in Imagism, which is considered old-fashioned now, I suppose, but it's still central to twentieth-century poetry. I read Pound's *Cathay* and then got on to other translations. As I learned more about it, I began to feel a kinship with the Chinese poets, who were all scholars and government officials."

"Are you a scholar?"

"I set out to be."

"What kind?"

"History."

"Then how did you end up as a civil servant?"

"By accident. Everything important happens by accident, doesn't it?"

"That's the theory of aleatoric art."

"But accidents are more than sheer randomness. Chance is the necessary condition for free choice. The Chinese cast lots and interpret them from the *I Ching*. In the west, we have traditions like the *sortes virgilianae*, or random opening of the Bible. The words open the mind to a new range of possibilities."

"Another of the things I noticed when I came to dinner is that I like to listen to you talk. You use words with . . . such care."

"My business, I suppose."

"As a poet?"

"And as a civil servant."

"Really?"

"Yes."

"I always thought their job was to say nothing and sound like they were saying something."

"That's a cynic's definition of a politician's job. A

civil servant's job is to make complicated issues and choices as clear as possible."

"You're good at that?"

"Yes."

"You didn't tell me how you ended up there."

"I was doing graduate work in history. The government forestry people were looking for someone to do the background research for a history of government policies on forestry in Ontario. I'd reached the point where I didn't want to go on with graduate study unless I could go away, and I couldn't go away."

"Why not?"

"My mother . . . It's not easy to explain. She was a difficult person, extraordinary, wounded, special. My brother and I both recognized that. We'd agreed that she couldn't be . . . abandoned."

Ray put the drinks on the table. Arnold thanked him, and he moved quietly away.

"What about your father?" Elena said.

"They were divorced. He was remarried."

"He abandoned her."

"My brother would say so."

"So you couldn't leave or get married."

"Nothing that unhealthy, Elena. I got married. I went away on trips. But I didn't feel I could leave Toronto permanently. After I did the job for the forestry people, I was offered a place in the government service. I thought I'd like it. By then I'd begun to publish poetry, and I thought the work might give me time to write."

"Just like the Chinese poets."

"I didn't think about it then, but yes."

Arnold sipped his whisky and looked out the window. Darkness had fallen. Fallen? Did it fall, or did it come up out of the earth? Or did light simply withdraw, leaving an absence that we chose to call darkness? The black air was vivid, with rain glittering around every fragment of light.

"Why am I talking about myself so much?" Arnold said.

"Because I asked."

There was something odd, stylized about her face, a sensual mouth, and above it, a thin straight nose, quick eyes; a hint of some inherent contradiction.

"When I saw you sketching," he said, "I was behind you, and I thought at first you were Chinese. You have Chinese hair."

"You have a Chinese career, and I have Chinese hair."

"Something about it like silk."

"Julia wants it for one of her puppets."

"Do you like her puppets?"

"Yes. I think they're brilliant. Do you?"

"They disturb me."

"They're meant to."

He drank and looked at her, and she met his eyes.

"During the T'ang dynasty," he said, "the examination for those who wished to enter the government service included the composition of a poem in a very strict form."

> *Nine splendid horses*
> *closed-matched in god-like metal.*
> *Their glances proud, free;*
> *their spirits firm and deep-seated.*

The pedestrian translation of the lines by Tu Fu is printed on a card in one of the glass cases. Another card explains that the Heavenly Horses of the T'ang dynasty were rare, valuable, exotic, brought long distances from the secret mountains in the heart of Turkestan.

"Can I see your drawing of the ceramic horses sometime?"

"I did several."

"I'd like to see them all."

"They're right here in my bag."

"Did you bring them to show me?"

"I always carry my sketchbook."

She passed it to him. He turned the pages.

"They're beautiful."

"It's hard to find a style that's appropriate and not just derivative."

"I've often thought of doing some poems with a Chinese background. The same problem."

"I loved the scrolls in your apartment."

"Come and see them again."

"I'd like to."

"I admire these drawings. We might do a book together, poems and drawings."

"Are you serious?"

"Don't you think it's a good idea?"

On the street, the July afternoon was hot and close, the city sunk in a damp haze that dimmed the outlines of the tall buildings, but inside the museum, it was cool. The artifacts were distant and perfect and welcoming. Arnold was standing in the exact spot where he had stood on that chilly afternoon when the sub-zero within him had told him that Marie was dying.

He was to meet Elena here, but he could not find her. Perhaps she would not come. He went and stood by the Ming tomb. A young couple entered the room.

They had a tiny baby which hung in a carrier against the man's chest, one of those soft cloth carriers that hadn't been invented (or reinvented from some primitive model) when Julia was born. These parents were both rather small, delicate-looking. Their child was a whole unlived history. Arnold felt suddenly that the air was too rich in oxygen, that it might sear his lungs. Possibilities, the future, poured over him like a waterfall.

It was years ago. He and Marie were in New York, and one afternoon, in the Frick, he had wandered out of the galleries into the courtyard, with its fountains and plants, and across the quiet space, he saw a man and a woman on a bench, a man in middle age, the woman younger, and just as Arnold looked across, the woman stood and walked away, then stopped and looked backward over her shoulder. She was tall, and stood with an easy elegance as she stared back at the man she was leaving, and he met her eyes, but the two of them remained perfectly still. It was impossible to be sure of what was happening between them, but it seemed intense, poignant, dangerous. Arnold turned away and went back into the gallery and studied the remarkable small Vermeer, "Girl Interrupted at her Music," with its brilliant, intricate rendering of light and its odd and puzzling pictorial convention, the girl looking straight at the viewer, as if this spectator has interrupted her, arriving from the future to provoke that mysterious, cool, assessing glance, the man who is with her still isolated inside the pictorial world, pointing out something in the music, something to which the girl will return in the imaginary moment that comes just after this, and which will never come.

Later, when Arnold walked back through the courtyard with Marie, the man and woman he had seen were gone.

"I've been working on a poem."
  "What's it about?"
  "It seems to be about old age."
  "Why? You're not old."
  "I will be, soon enough."
  "Do you want to be old?"
  "Would anyone?"
  "There's something stable about it. It gives you a clear position. Just declare yourself a wise old man, and a lot of things aren't expected of you."
  "You amaze me," he said.
  "Why?"
  "The things you see."
  "Lots of people see things. I've trained myself to say them out loud."
  "Do you still like the scrolls?"
  "Especially the calligraphy."
  "The brushstroke is the central act of both their painting and calligraphy."
  "That's why it makes sense to have writing on the paintings."
  "One painter wrote that the single brushstroke was the origin of all existence."
  "What's that poem about?"
  "Autumn. Wang Wei wonders whether his sadness will ever come to an end."
  "Is that real sadness or just poetic sadness?"
  "Hard to know. He was a Buddhist and something of a mystic."
  "I'd like to learn Chinese calligraphy. I should poke around Dundas Street and find somebody to teach me."

"They say it takes years to learn."

"When are you going to finish your new poem?"

"I write very slowly. By the time I've finished work and come home and made something to eat, I often feel there's nothing left."

She was very still, concentrating on the scrolls on the wall in front of her.

"*La chinoise*," he said. "That's the phrase that came into my head when I saw you in the museum."

"Because of my hair."

"I'd like to brush your hair," he said. "It would be like brushing silk."

He hadn't planned the words, hadn't expected them. He felt revealed and humiliated.

"Would that make a poem?" she said.

The beautifully sculpted bodies of the horses are the more moving because they are made of ceramic, baked and glazed clay that can be shattered by a single hammer blow. Tomb offerings, they were created to carry the spirit of greatness into the country of death.

There was a cool breeze as they walked through Queen's Park. The city went on its way around them in the September night, swarming and multiple, but when they sat on a bench, there was a kind of stillness. One could imagine the wings of birds moving through the high darkness.

"Why did you ever stop writing?"

"I'm not sure I can say."

"Did it have anything to do with your wife's death?"

"No. It happened long before that. In fact since she died, I've been in the grip of something that feels like a need to write, even though it doesn't ever find expression. The day I realized that she was going to die, something went cold inside me, a physical cold at first, but even when that disappeared, there was something else, something chilled and distant. Something that wanted to be put into language."

"Did you try to write?"

"Yes, but the words seemed unnatural, unnecessary."

"But now you're writing a little."

"Yes."

"Why did you never learn Chinese?"

"It was a plan for the future. To do it properly, not just memorize a few characters. And then go to China. Marie and I used to talk about a trip to China. After she got sick, it was a talisman against the illness, against the possibility of death."

"Do you think you'll go now?"

"It doesn't seem likely. I have a dilettante's interest in Chinese poetry and art, but after Mao, the Cultural Revolution, all the campaigns to modernize—what do I really know? For me, China is a poet's fancy. Such things can't be seen on tour and photographed. The distance is half the fascination."

"But now you're writing again. Anything's possible."

"Have you found someone to teach you Chinese calligraphy?"

"Not yet, but I bought some brushes and inks to experiment with. Did you know that most of the early artists painted when they were drunk? There was one who spread out silk on the floor and splashed it with ink. Like an action painter."

"Are you interested in the action painters? Aren't they out of date now?"

"I don't care about that. I've always liked the ones with the big black brushstrokes on white. Franz Kline. I think I've been ready for Chinese art for years. I've always loved ink."

The wind was getting colder now. She shoved her hands into the pockets of the old suit jacket she was wearing. Her head was bent forward.

"I can't get used to your hair being short," he said.

"Julia needed it."

"It's very generous of you to cut your beautiful hair for her."

The air was sharp with frost.

"Are you pleased to be going away?" he said.

"Pleased to be planning it. I sometimes think half the fun of travel is the planning."

"I suppose the book we talked about won't happen."

"It's six weeks till we leave. I can do the drawings and leave them with you."

"Yes. We don't want direct illustrations."

She looked toward him as she walked at his side.

"I'm paying my own way, you know," she said.

"Why do you say that?"

"I didn't want you to think that Julia was throwing away her legacy taking me to Europe."

"It's her money, Elena. I can understand that she wouldn't want to travel alone. And I'm sure that you wouldn't do anything that wasn't honourable."

"Honourable. That's not a word I've ever thought of applying to myself. I guess it isn't a word I'd use."

"I suppose I'm sometimes old-fashioned."

"Yes. I like it."

"I'll miss you when you go away."

"You'll have the drawings to make into a book."

"I've been thinking about Wang Wei as a subject for one of the poems."

"A poem about a poet?"

"He was a poet and artist both. But none of his paintings survives. All we have left is possible copies from lost originals. But sometimes we have the poem that went with the painting. Maybe all I have is a title. 'Lost Originals.'"

"Are you shivering?"

"There's a chill in the air since the sun's gone down."

"October, or the cold inside you again?"

"A little of both."

"Thinking about Marie?"

"No. Thinking about you."

"I'm not dying."

"No, but you're going away. I say things to you that I don't say to anyone else."

She took his arm.

"Stop shivering."

"Yes," he said. "I will. As soon as we get inside."

"Do you shiver at work?"

"Lord no. That would never do. I'm in a responsible position. It would undermine my authority."

"Of course," she said, "your self-control is perfect."

"Yes."

At the top of the scroll, a distant peak, and falling away from it, eroded hills flecked with tiny strokes of ink, a little thin vegetation on the treeless slopes. Halfway down the scroll, a stream appears and tumbles over rocks, past bare cliffs, into the foreground. The landscape is constructed with long sinuous strokes of the brush, and the weight of the hills at the top of the long vertical scroll bears down. They hang, precarious, and the water of the stream falls precipitously. The only trees are those which rise from the bare rocks near the bottom and are themselves bare, or thinly leaved. The topmost branches of the tallest trees just reach the gap where the stream appears out of the cliffs. Below, where the stream narrows into rapids, a single figure, a man with a staff, walks toward a bridge.

As he approaches the wooden bridge, the traveller listens to the tumult of the stream dropping down the narrow gorge. Leaves fall in the water and disappear. He remembers other hills. He hears the desolate sound of wind. Ahead of him is a long mountainous road.

Outside the old-fashioned leaded windows, the air was full of snowflakes, a light but persistent accumulation that had begun a few minutes before, as the two of them were sitting with the small bowls of tea in their hands. As Arnold watched the movement of the tiny white flakes, a movement that seemed to have some perceptible and yet inexplicable pattern, he could hear Elena preparing herself. Was there, he wondered, some beautiful mathematical equation that could encapsulate the movement of the multitudinous flakes? Or was it one of those cases where the pattern was in the seeing, an illusion created by mind and brain, which could not contain randomness and changed it, inevitably, into form? He turned around.

Elena had folded back the small carpet to make space for her materials and had unrolled a long scroll of fine paper and put weights at the corners to hold it flat on the patterned wood floor, and now she was setting up her brushes and inks on a piece of newspaper. She was wearing black trousers, tight at the ankle, and a loose purple shirt, unbuttoned, over a black T-shirt. The short hair made her look smaller and quicker.

"What made you think of this?" he said.

"I wanted to leave you something—besides those little drawings for the book—and I've been playing around with Chinese inks for quite a while. You got me started."

"Can you talk while you work?"

"Sometimes. If I can't answer, I won't."

She had the materials all set out in front of her, and she was kneeling in front of the scroll, her body back on her heels, her spine very straight, studying the paper.

"You look as if you might be praying."

"Thinking," she said. "Waiting."

"Contemplation," he said. "The secular name for prayer."

He returned to the window, and the snow was still falling, but thinly enough that he could see the lights of the high towers beyond. There was a hissing in the radiator, a shapeless, continuous noise that resonated softly in his ears. He could hear the soft sounds of movement behind him, a murmur now and then. Arnold was engaged in a contest with himself to see how long he could wait before looking back at her. He wanted to watch every movement she made, the way her fingers curled around the brush.

It had to be admitted how much he wished to touch her. He never had, not even the sociable gesture of patting a hand or shoulder, which might have been misconstrued, might have been something cheap. Once or twice she had taken his arm, and each time, it had been like an electric shock. Now, like Orpheus, he turned. Her brush was racing up one side of the page to create a long bamboo stalk. She was so young and beautiful, her quick hands so clever. Had he been less proud, he might have reached out his hands to caress her. He might have told her how beautiful she was.

"Are you all packed for the trip?" he said.

"I think so. I keep unpacking and reorganizing things. It's hard to keep the pack light enough for mobility and still be ready for all kinds of weather."

"Julia seems convinced that she can buy clothes when she needs them and abandon them when she doesn't."

"I think having some extra money has gone to her head."

"Do you?"

"Don't sound so worried and fatherly. I don't think it's serious. She's not going to spend it all in the first week. Just a little holiday from frugality."

She had changed brushes, and now her hands were moving in quick jerks, setting leaves on the bamboo. Her eyes were concentrated, her soft lips open.

"Is your family worrying over you going away?"

"Not much. They're preoccupied with my brother's latest disaster."

"What's that?"

"Car accident. Drunk. No insurance."

"He's always in trouble, isn't he?"

"He does his best to be. Actually that's my younger brother. My older brother hasn't been in trouble for at least six months."

Invisible at home, she came to him for interest and approval. Proud, honourable, prudent, reticent, he didn't take advantage of that, not in the most obvious ways, at least. He didn't invite her into his bed.

Once again she had changed brushes, and now her hands danced over the paper in the chopping and

swooping strokes of Chinese ideograms. He was fascinated by the movement, the swiftness, how white her
hands were, how white all her skin must be; but even
so, there was something oriental about her, the size,
the daintiness. *La chinoise.* Why did he always think it
in French? It was less real, more a part of the world of
artifice. The world where he knew her was the world
of the museum; the eternal beauty of things made
with the hands to outlast the body that made them.

He had almost begun to believe that their book
might really come to be. The drawings would stay
with him, the memory. It was better not to try to make
her real.

The characters she was drawing were filling their
corner of the scroll. The bamboo and the Chinese
calligraphy hung in space. Her brush slashed downward in a final stroke, and she stood up and looked
toward him, her eyes bright with the excitement of
what she had done.

11

The needle vibrated in his fingers, and the vibration passed up his arm, into the stack of little bone doughnuts that was his spine, and from there into the brain, which made every nerve in his body sizzle with tiny, quick oscillations. His eyes were focussed, and yet unseeing; he was distant and untouchable, cast in steel, and yet also he was closely present, aware of every detail of the body that lay beneath him, at his mercy. The tuft of fine blonde pubic hair that stuck straight out from her belly: there was a pathos about it. It was so girlish and ridiculous. As she lay on her side, he could see the arched bones of her ribs beneath the pale ivory slipcover of the skin, and beneath the upward curve of the last rib, the flesh lifted and fell with short quick breaths, a little flutter of pain and panic, the pain caused by the needle that buzzed in his fingers, buzzed in his brain. The soft flesh of her hip welled with blood as the needle ate away at it, penetrating the epidermis, staining it with dye, his left hand on her thigh, supporting her, holding her still, until he moved it to one side, picked up a piece of gauze and wiped the traces of blood off the skin.

"It hurts, Donald," she said.

"Nearly done, Rat."

"I'm crazy to let you do this."

"Yes, you are."

He bent over the little snake that he was tattooing on her soft skin, at the side of the hip where it would be hidden by underwear or a bathing suit, visible only when she was naked. It needed only a little more detail on the head. He looked up at her face. The eyes were closed, and her lips were drawn back, making the slight protuberance of the upper teeth more prominent. There was a dark mole under her chin. Her small breasts pointed irrelevantly off into the room, the nipples shrivelled and tight.

His stomach was raw and sore. A grey emptiness inside him. He wanted to turn and run. The freedom in her, or daring, or passivity, or desperation, whatever it was, the feeling that he could do anything to her, frightened him. He was close to hating her. He was in over his head.

His needle drove into her flesh, and his fingers scrolled the shape of the long, curving, forked tongue. The red, terrible tongue. A tiny sub-tongue of blood ran beside it, and he wiped it away with gauze. He looked at her face, and there was a dampness of tears on the short brown eyelashes. Why didn't she stop him? But she never did. He'd taken her to the empty house on Major Street, and undressed her and laid her down on the bare, dusty floor, and as they moved on each other, half-stunned, wincing, their cries tiny in the deserted rooms, Donald could feel the emptiness of the house and beyond that the emptiness of space, himself out there, oxygen-starved, staring back at the two naked bodies finally lapsed into satiety and still as the dead. She had sucked him into a zone of silence where he could not recognize himself. The words he spoke in his own head meant nothing.

At night he jerked up, blind awake, from dreams in which she begged him to kill her, and in the morning, he would leave the house early and go to her bed, as if he might finish it there, achieve a completion that would leave them free. It was time for her to go away, to marry, to make a life.

A month ago, he had suggested she leave, move away. He offered to pay six months' rent somewhere else. It was the only time he had seen her cry, wantonly, savagely, because he had offered her money to go, and so he had eaten his words, apologized.

But it was the only way, to have her far off, someplace where he could not find her. Otherwise he would feel the dreadful hint of possibilities creeping through his brain, over his skin, and he would arrive at her door, and the two of them would laugh and attempt the old jokes, but it would only be an imitation of the time when they were tough and easy.

As she lay beneath his hands now, her thin arm was lifted, the hand pressed against the side of her head. A bit of fine straight hair in the narrow hollow of the armpit, the shoulder blade canted, protruding. She was so bare and helpless.

Donald switched off the needle and set it aside, took up a tube of ointment and rubbed it over the tattooed area, then taped on a piece of gauze. The fingers of his small hands were dark and fat against her pale skin and small bones. She turned on her back and spread her legs.

"Now you have to make me feel better. You have to make up for hurting me."

Donald wanted to say no, but his body was not in agreement, and he uncovered himself and joined her.

"Will it last forever?" she said, as he entered her. "The mark you put on me?"

"It will last as long as you last, Rat."

"So when I'm an old lady I can show it to my grandchildren."

"If you like."

"My skin will be all loose and shrivelled like old women get, and I'll pull up my nightie, and they'll be awful shocked and I'll tell them how when I was young, a man made me do it."

"I didn't make you do it."

"Yes you did. You made me do it, and you hurt me."

"It always hurts a little."

"You hurt me, Duck. You made me do it, and you hurt me, and you made a mark on me forever."

As he moved inside her, Donald was thinking about his father, how he had run away from Sandra and drowned himself. Had Sandra been like this for him, an intoxication, a drug, something he couldn't escape, that took away his will? Donald had tried, in his own stupid way, to be decent. Half-way decent, to Daphne at least. It came hard; it wasn't natural, but he tried.

"You got to screw me awful good, Duck, to make up for putting a mark on me forever."

He pulled back, yanked his penis out of her; he shuddered with the shock and she cried out as he lifted his body away.

"I don't have to do anything, Rat. I don't *have* to."

His voice was furious.

Then she was looking at him with her light, hot

eyes, and stroking him with her hands, and he was back inside her, and he was swimming somewhere in an ocean with no floor.

An hour later, downstairs in his office, he was playing back the tape on the answering machine. He heard a complaint about a broken lock, a request to renew a lease, something that sounded like a failed attempt at an obscene call, and then he was hearing Daphne's voice. While he had been upstairs, hypnotized and sickened and delighted, she had been calling him, complaining about the answering machine, as she always did, and telling him, her voice edgy, abrupt, that he had got a call at home from some woman named Jeanie who had started to cry.

Jeanie.

Not now, not now, not now.

Footsteps came down the stairs, and he saw the Rat pass in front of the window of the tattoo parlour. She didn't look in, and he knew it was deliberate, but wasn't sure what it meant. It was a cold grey day, threatening rain or snow, and as she walked away, his brain was tattooed with the image of her body, dressed in the yellow uniform, a leather jacket over top, the little hips pushing her feet over the pavement, the tattoo, bandaged in gauze, hidden beneath skirt and pantyhose. The mark he had left on her forever. For a moment, he saw a little body, naked and helpless, in the hands of an undertaker, who only half-noticed the tattoo, incurious, and Donald was seized by vertigo, so dizzy he had to hold the edge of the desk for support. He hung on, waited.

The door opened. There was someone near him. He couldn't quite make out who it was. The face was almost familiar. It was someone he should know, but he was still half-dizzy, and paralyzed and stupid. He couldn't move or comprehend. There was something wrong with his brain. He'd have to have an operation, a brain transplant. Things wouldn't hold still or make sense.

"Are you all right?" she was saying. "You look sick."

"No," he said, "I'm fine. Dizzy for a minute. I'm probably getting the flu."

He could see her now. It was Arnold's daughter. In a minute he'd remember her name.

"Why don't you sit down?" she said. "You don't look very good."

Julia.

"I'm OK."

"Sit down."

He did.

"Surprise," he said. "You being sympathetic."

"Don't worry," she said. "As soon as you look a little better, I'll be nasty again."

"You're not as tough as you let on."

"Are you?"

"I always thought so."

"I always figured Daphne was the really tough one. Under it all."

He didn't want her talking about Daphne, not while he could still feel the slippery sweetness of the Rat on his flesh, still remember the vigour with which his body had emptied itself into her.

"You want a coffee?" he said.

"No. I have to get back."

"Your father says you're going to Europe."

"In a month or so."

"So you're giving me notice?"

"I thought maybe you'd have some place I could store my stuff. I don't know when I'll be back, and there's too much for the apartment."

"I might have."

His words meant nothing. He couldn't think straight, even yet, but if he sat here for a minute, staring at the familiar plain face, thought might once more begin to take place in the cells of his festering brain.

Jeanie didn't look that much different. Not really. She'd taken care of herself. The hair was a little darker, some kind of rinse hiding the grey. She was maybe a little heavier, but she was a clean, proper, decent, respectable woman, and she was, undeniably, Jeanie, who'd been a girl when he last saw her, and his lover. He knew her too well. He didn't know what to say. When she arrived at the door after dinner, he had brought her into the house, taken the tweed coat and hung it up, then led the way into the living-room, where Daphne sat in the stuffed chair beside the case of Doulton, her face ominously still. He thought, as he introduced the two women, that there was something soft about Jeanie, something vulnerable, a mouth that seemed a little too quick, too delicate, the hint of a slight cast to her eyes that gave her face an exotic look. She had never been pretty, but she was beautiful. The way her eyes met his momentarily, the appeal in them. For what? Kindness? Protection?

"It's been a long time," Donald said. The line was meant for Daphne, who was sitting back in her chair, pale and stiff. To tell her that Jeanie was a voice from the distant past, before her time. False reassurance, he supposed, given with the smell of the Rat still on his body, a few tiny drops of blood still oozing from the mark he had made on her.

"Eighteen years," Jeanie said. "Eighteen years last summer."

"I have some orders to finish down at the store,"

Daphne said. She moved forward in her chair, as if to leave.

"I'll drive you down later on," Donald said. Whatever it was, let them face it now, rather than having Daphne turn up later, silent, wanting an explanation but refusing to ask. He knew those silences.

"Walter's in town," Jeanie said. "My husband. At a conference."

Donald tried to remember if her voice had always been shaped by those flat American vowels. Waaalltuhr. Couldn't recall. Perhaps, whispering in bed, they were less noticeable.

"I felt I had to come to see you. I had to. After it happened, I kept thinking about you, and thinking that I had to let you know."

Donald glanced toward Daphne who looked like something carved in snow, her eyes unnaturally dark in the pale soft face. Pieces of coal inserted in the white hollows. Perhaps he should have let her leave, dealt with it later. Too late now. He was shivering a little, as if the temperature in the room had plunged, and yet his face was hot, flushed. He was in a trap, and he had to control the panic, or the jaws of the trap would gnaw more deeply into his flesh. Look it in the face. Make it happen.

"It's about the boy," he said.

"Yes," Jeanie said.

Donald turned to his wife.

"After she went back to the States," he said, "eighteen years ago, Jeanie had a baby. I guess it was mine, I mean, it was, it was mine."

Daphne's face turned, just an inch or two away, to avoid his eyes, then she was still again. He could hear Jeanie's voice.

"He's dead, Donald. Phillip's dead. It was in a car. I

think maybe he'd had something to drink. You know, teenage boys. He lost control, and the car hit the side of a building. The doctor said it was over in seconds. He didn't suffer. The doctor swore to me he didn't suffer."

She was crying softly, as if the tears were familiar now, old friends whose presence no longer frightened her. Donald's whole body seemed to be compressed, in need of escape from this room but helpless to move, screaming.

"He was a good boy. He really was. Walter and I had great hopes for him."

Waaaltuhr.

"When did it happen?" Donald said.

"In the spring," Jeanie said. "He was just about set to graduate high school, and they were all so busy with plans for the summer, and college in the fall. It was a real happy time. Phillip and Walter were planning a fishing trip for August. It seemed like a real happy time, and then this officer came to the door, and I knew it right away from the look on his face. Elizabeth Anne, she's my daughter, she came up behind me while he was standing there, and all I could do was say for her to go upstairs and wait. I knew I had to face it alone first of all."

She stopped speaking, and Donald became aware that his own breathing was all he could hear. Resonant, thunderous.

"They got me through it, Walter and Elizabeth Anne, and our friends. They got me through it. But you're never the same. I won't ever be the same as I was, but I have the two of them to look after, and they're good to me. You just have to go on with it. I knew that. But I got to thinking about you, Donald, and I felt that I had to let you know. You weren't ready for a baby in those days, I could understand that, at least I tried, and when Phillip was born, before Walter came along, you were good about helping out. I just felt I had to tell you. But I didn't know where you were living now. I wasn't even sure that you were still here in Toronto. Then Walter mentioned this conference, and I told him I'd like to come and see if I could find you, just to let you know."

Donald knew he had to respond. But he had no words.

"It was very thoughtful of you to come," Daphne was saying.

"Yes," Donald said. He looked toward Daphne, who still avoided his eyes.

Jeanie reached into the pocket of her dress and took out a picture.

"I wondered if you might like to have this." She held it out. Donald went and took it. A picture of a smiling boy. He couldn't take in anything else about it. He put it in the pocket of his shirt.

"I wouldn't have intruded before," Jeanie said. "I know it would have seemed like I was asking for something, but now, he's gone, and I thought you should know."

Donald was staring down at her, all his attention focussed on the soft, beautiful face. He wanted to touch her. He remembered that the pale brown hair was very fine and soft to touch. But his hands stayed at his sides. He could feel the stiff paper of the photograph against his chest. He tried to remember the boy's face. Couldn't. Did it look like his? He knew he should be saying something, but his tongue was locked.

Jeanie stood up. He wanted to hug her. He wanted to tell her they would run away together. He wanted her to be gone. He wanted her never to have come. She was too soft, too vulnerable. He hated that softness.

"Thanks," he said, "for finding me."

"I called a couple of your old friends. It wasn't hard."

They walked toward the door. Daphne didn't move from her chair.

"I'm sorry," she said, standing, suddenly, and walking toward Jeanie. "I'm sorry for your grief."

They stood still, awkward. Donald took down the tweed coat and held it for Jeanie to put on. He opened the door for her. She was close beside him, and the odd, slightly cast eyes were holding him, with a kind of tenderness. She smiled.

"Jeanie," he said. She was out the door and walking down the front steps into the night. He watched for a second and then closed the door behind her.

When he walked back into the living-room, Daphne was standing with her back to him, staring into the stiff bright landscape of the Doulton figurines, as still as if she might have been one of them, a part of that perfected ceramic world. Donald stopped just inside the door, unable to move any closer. The cold force of her hostility held him off.

"You could have told me," she said.

"It was a long time ago. It was all over."

She drew open the glass door of the case and took out one of the china figures, a dainty-faced woman in a long pale blue dress and matching bonnet. She held it gently, carefully in her round, shapely hands.

"You knew how much I wanted a baby."

"We tried."

"You didn't even tell me that you had a son living somewhere in the States."

"I didn't think it mattered. It was all over with."

"You never really wanted a baby with me, did you?"

Her fingers were stroking the slippery glaze on the Doulton figure.

"I did everything I could."

"You wouldn't go to a doctor."

"I didn't figure I needed to."

"Rub it in, Donald. That's right. Rub it in. You gave her a baby, but you wouldn't give me one."

He could feel something gathering in her. It was like the slow empty moment before a storm broke. He wanted to be somewhere far off.

"I didn't give her a baby. It just happened. I didn't want it. That's why she left Toronto."

"It didn't just happen. Things don't just happen." She spoke softly, almost whispering. "If you really loved me, we would have had a baby. If you really wanted one. If you really wanted me to have your baby."

"Daph, that doesn't make sense."

"It makes sense. You'll never admit it, but it does. All those doctors, they were never sure there was anything wrong with me, were they? What was wrong with me was you. You didn't want a baby. You already had one with her. And you wouldn't tell me the truth, would you? You wouldn't tell me. You wouldn't."

She was starting to sob. Donald moved toward her, and when he did, she turned and threw the figurine. He pulled to one side, and it hit the doorway behind him and smashed, and after it had fallen in pieces, Daphne began to take the others out of the case and smash them, deliberately, one after the other against the dark walnut frame of the glass display case he had made for her.

"You never tell me the truth. How many children do you have with your other women? You think I don't know about the other women? Do you think I can't smell them on you?" Her face was red and swollen, and she was sobbing and smashing the delicate shiny figures that they had collected with such care over so many years. She reached in and took out the old lady with the balloons, the first one he'd bought her, cheap, from a thief, and she smashed it. Cheap, from a thief. Long ago. The head fell to the carpet and stared up at him with bright idiotic eyes. The sound of Daphne's sobs was getting louder, deafening him to everything else. The bright eyes of the china head hypnotized him. With an effort of will, he broke loose and walked out of the house.

Donald sat in the dark and waited. Until he was ready, though he couldn't guess when that would be. Earlier he had gone through the files and taken out a handful of the most important cards, put them in an envelope, addressed them to himself, at the house, and put stamps on the envelope. It sat in his jacket pocket, to be dropped in the mail after he left. The street outside was empty, high poles and long curbs lit from above by streetlights. Down on the Danforth, traffic passed in a steady stream. People going somewhere.

He listened for sounds from above, from the Rat's apartment, but he heard nothing. Maybe she was out for the night, sleeping with some attractive stranger she'd met in a bar. A knife twisted in the space behind his ribs.

No one had seen him arrive here, and since he'd come in, he'd kept the lights off, and stayed away from the windows. They wouldn't find any evidence of his presence. When the cards came in the mail, he could hide them away, and no one else would know where they had come from.

Anyone who looked in the window would see nothing. He wasn't here. Nobody was here. There could be no evidence against him.

The Rat was away. She must be. It was too early for her to be asleep, unless she had come home drunk and passed out. Even so she'd be sure to wake in time. Sure to. Most likely, she was in some strange bed, not here. She was sitting astride some lean, well-hung kid, pronged on his big thing, her straight hair hanging down toward his face, her breasts swallowed in his hands.

Donald had small hands. It was something he'd always hated about himself, that he'd inherited his mother's small hands. And maybe her craziness as well.

Arnold, his father, they were so calm, always in control, but he was like his mother, flustered, impulsive, dazed. His whole life had been a battle to hold things together when every moment they seemed on the point of flying apart, into fragments. The way he had let the Rat get under his skin. His terrible need to put that tattoo on her; the knowledge that he could have her in his power and yet, doing it, be more naked, weaker, than he had ever been before. He had recognized the disease and reached out for the infection. Had his father been like that with Sandra? No, he hadn't. For sure. His father was not half-crazed, not ever. Sandra had given him something he wanted, and he had taken it. And Arnold. Arnold had planned his life the way he might plan a poem, and he had selected Marie because she fit the plan; she rhymed.

Daphne hadn't even liked him much, not at first.

Even there, he had been out of control, struggling to catch her interest. To prove himself to her. He would hang around the furniture store where she worked, bragging about his properties, about how much money he was going to make. It was hard to find excuses to go to the store, but he made up the most transparent ones, hardly caring that she could see through them, that she might feel only contempt for him. He had to go, he had to talk, he had to impress her. It was so that he could brag to her about it that he bought the apartment building where Arnold lived now. He couldn't afford it, and for the next six months he was on the brink of bankruptcy, every payment late, lying to every mortgage holder about the extent of his indebtedness to others. He thought it would kill him, but somehow she came to understand that it was for her that he had done this, wrecked his nerves. She was protective. She seemed almost to like him. In bed, she gentled him, taught him to be less rough and eager. With Jeanie, when he arrived, late and crazed, it was just Scotch and music, and quick to bed, the edges blurred, but Daphne stood face to face with him, made him slow down, trust her.

He had failed her. He had never let himself realize how much of a thing it was to her to have a child. But even then, what could he have done? He had poured out his sperm in her. On impulse or on the basis of her calculations. It had been good enough to get Jeanie knocked up after one night of drunken carelessness. He wondered if Daphne could be right, that he had been too frightened of giving her a child, frightened of the power she would have over him then. He didn't know. He didn't know anything. Except that when he went back to her, tomorrow, he would be free. He would burn away the infection. He would give the

Rat money, anything she needed. He'd see to it she was all right, but somewhere else. A place he couldn't find.

Outside the window a car went past, silently rolling its wheels through some other world, a world he no longer inhabited. There were too many clocks running in his head, one slow clock, with every second delayed, moments forced into being with a shudder that shook his whole body, and beside it another clock, or if not beside it, behind it, underneath, a clock that unrolled years of the past, years of the future, and a third clock, plodding along mechanically, the pendulum waving back and forth, back and forth. He was waiting for a moment when all the three clocks would speak to him in a single voice and tell him it was time, now, to do it and go.

His car was parked several blocks away, on a street where no one would know him or recognize the car.

He listened, trying to make out if there was any hint of sound from upstairs, but all he could hear was the traffic on the Danforth, the tiny sounds of the old building growing older, the beating of his heart, his breath. His hearing could not penetrate through the floor. He needed the powers of a comic book hero to see into the apartment above. Superman.

As a boy he always hid his comic books from his mother. They were secret and richly sexual. In the privacy of his room, Donald drew nipples on the big breasts of Betty and Veronica. He speculated on how Superman couldn't ever marry Lois Lane because his super hard-on would tear her to shreds. He had to conceal these things from his mother, the dim, sumptuous, sickened passions of this private world. Already, he knew, she felt a faint disgust for him, his heavy awkwardness, and he would not add to her burdens. He would keep it to himself, this swamp of prurience in which he lay, lathered and panting.

The telephone rang, and he cried out loud, with shock, but the machine answered it and began its routine announcement, and he sat perfectly still, as if the tiny voice was speaking to him, telling him something of crucial importance.

Perhaps it was a message for him, telling him it was time to act. He waited until the machine had shut itself off, and then he went into the front room of the tattoo parlour, put several needles in the dental sterilizer, added a miniscule amount of water, and plugged it in. The water would boil away within a few minutes, and the sterilizer would begin to overheat. It had been dangerous for months. On the shelf beside it was a plastic container of methyl hydrate. The quick blue flames would start here and run up the wall. Old paint, old wall-paper, well-dried joists. It would catch fire quickly. He didn't need to burn the place to the ground. Just enough to make the apartment upstairs uninhabitable. Just bad enough that she would have to go, disappear and never come back. He put in the plug.

The act was done, and he walked to the front door, looked for signs of men, women, observers, saw none and left, vanishing up the street toward his hidden car.

Once in the car, moving, he felt free, confident, and he made his way through traffic like a fish through the intricacies of a coral reef, lights passing overhead in a rhythmic sequence, houses, an unexplained pattern of dark and light, street, lanes, alleys providing a multiplicity of possible turns, and he took them, a left, a right, at random, and in front of him was a lighted corner, a used car lot, with a pay phone on the sidewalk beside it, and he was stopped, out of the car, and dialling the Rat's phone number. It rang. Rang. Rang. Rang. Rang. Rang. Rang. Nothing. He hung up. She was unconscious on the bed, had staggered in drunk and was in too deep a sleep to hear the telephone. He dialled again, in case he'd made a mistake before. It rang. Rang. Rang. Rang. Rang. Nothing.

She couldn't be there. She couldn't be that drunk. It was still early. She was out on the town, smoking dope, getting laid. She was OK. The Rat was tough. She'd always be OK. When the strange man who took her to bed asked about the bandage on her hip, she'd make a joke, take off the bandage and show him the little snake. They'd have a good laugh over it.

Donald could feel the fine shuddering of the tattoo needle in his arms. Saw the bony body, the tight little nipples. The traces of blood that he wiped away. Flames all around her. She jumped from the bed, naked and confused, and ran toward the door, lost, striking a blind wall, her cries inaudible in the snapping and roaring of the flames, eager, well-started now.

He pulled over, got out of the car, walked, found himself at the east end of the Bloor Viaduct, which hung in the air over the Don Valley. Far below him the lights of the cars flowed both ways, and to one side, the river was a dark oily surface as it moved to lose itself in the lake. His body was shaking. Cars passed close behind him on the bridge, and the wind of their passing blew his hair. Headlights revealed him. As he looked down to the valley, his breath came faster. He imagined the stone railing beginning to crumble, saw himself falling through the dark air.

He turned and walked off the bridge, tried to find his car. It was lost, and then it was in front of him.

Could he go back to the house, help Daphne clean up the mess on the floor, try to talk to her about his son? His dead son. No, he couldn't do that. But he must go somewhere, get himself off the road.

"What's the matter?"
   "Nothing's the matter."
   "Something's bothering you."
   "Just get me a drink."
Arnold went to the kitchen and got some ice, poured Scotch over it in two glasses and went back. His brother was sitting still in a chair, looking like someone who had been told to sit still in a chair. Arnold handed him the drink.
   "Julia left some stuff in the place she was renting," Donald said. "I'll bring it around sometime."
   "What kind of things?"
   "Just books, a jacket, a couple of tools."
   "She should have cleaned the place up."
   "Yes."
   "You want me to come and help?"
   "No."
   "You're drinking that Scotch like it was water."
   "I like the taste."
   "Am I supposed to ignore the state you're in?"
   "Might as well. Can't do anything about it."
   "It's about this woman. Who got under your skin."
   "Not any more."
   "It's over?"
   "It's going to be."
   "When?"
   "Soon."
   "You sent her a letter."
   "No."
   "What?"

"She lives over the tattoo parlour. I'm burning the place down."

"You're not serious, are you?"

"Then she'll have to move out."

"How are you planning to burn it down?"

"The sterilizer overheats. I left some methyl hydrate right beside it in a plastic bottle."

"You're serious, aren't you, Donald."

"Yes."

"What happens to her?"

"She's not there. I don't think she's there. The place is dark. I kept phoning. Except I keep thinking that she's too drunk or stoned to hear anything. But she's not there. I know she's not there."

"You better go back. Turn off the sterilizer. This is completely insane. It's the craziest thing you've ever done."

"You think so?"

"You have to go and stop it."

"It's too late. It's probably burning by now."

Arnold drank down the Scotch, walked to the window, turned and walked back. He did the same thing over again, then stopped and stood still.

"Where's your car?"

"Right out front."

Arnold went to the closet and took out a heavy tweed jacket.

"I'll go with you. We have to make sure she isn't there."

"She's not."

"Can you be sure?"

"No."

"Come on then."

"You don't have to do this, Arnold."

"I'm your brother. Let me do something for once."

Donald got up, and the two of them went out. Arnold insisted on driving. Donald gave him directions, and as they drove, he tried to imagine what Daphne had done after he left. She had phoned Sheldon Zemans, told him to come to her, and now the two of them were going at it on the floor among the broken pieces of china. Daphne was washing Donald's traces off her body with the sweat and semen of his enemy.

As they got close, Donald could see the reflection of a red flashing light on the windows of a flower shop. Arnold pulled to the side of the road.

"We're too late," he said.

"She couldn't have been there. I kept on phoning."

"I'll go and see."

Donald watched his brother going toward the figures who were gathered behind the trucks, men in helmets and long black rubber coats. He could smell the bitter smoke. He saw the Rat run screaming to the window, flames eating her hair, singeing her skin as she choked on the smoke. He saw Daphne spreading herself for that man. He looked toward the group of people on the street, garish red and black. He couldn't see his brother. Donald closed his eyes and waited.

The door of the car opened.

"They searched the apartment upstairs. There was no one there."

Arnold started the car and drove away. Donald couldn't open his eyes.

12

The box sat in the corner of the room, and in the box, the book, and in the book, the letter. When Donald came to the door with the carton of possessions that Julia had left behind when she put her things in storage, Arnold had taken it and set it near the door.

When his brother was gone, Arnold bent to pick up the box and put it away at the back of the clothes closet, but as he did, he saw, sticking out the end of a science fiction paperback, a letter in Elena's handwriting, and the words that caught his eye were *your father*. He stood, turned away from the box, and went to the window. He stood behind glass, and outside, beyond a curtain of falling snow, the lights of the city were glittering and unreal. He was a perfect eye, perfectly watching.

Julia and Elena were someplace in North Africa in pursuit of an exotic tradition of puppetry practised there. Eventually, Julia would send him a postcard, but she had made it quite clear before she left that he was not expected to worry about her or to expect frequent contact. She was an adult and capable and independent. He agreed; she was those things.

Since they had left, he had made it a practice, every day, to study the drawings Elena had made for him, the small ones and the large scroll, and to make notes. The actual writing, a line here and there, had begun, as if the voice in his head that spoke poetry was moving from its hiding place far off in a distant sky and proceeding toward him, now just within earshot.

The sight of Elena's handwriting, the knowledge that she had been thinking about him, writing about him, was intriguing, a little, almost, intoxicating. Yet he was too honourable a man, surely, to read someone else's letters. He was too honourable a man.

He walked back from the window and stood above the box, bent and touched the letter, and as he did, he could hear Elena's voice, see the face, the hair that Julia had cut short to provide for the needs of her puppets.

Instead of reading the letter, he should write about its mystery. It could be connected, in a metaphoric way, to the lost originals of Wang Wei. It could be part of that poem about lost things. He stood and went to the kitchen to make himself a drink. One of the radiators was knocking. The wind sang against the windows. He was closed inside a room inside a building. Invisible. The voice that spoke poetry was a long way off as he sipped the whisky and imagined Elena here, kneeling on the floor, painting the scroll for him. Her quick hands.

He went back to the other room, took out the letter and unfolded it.

Dearest Julia,

Some people like anger, think of it as one of the great passions, something fierce and intense. I don't. I don't want you to be mad at me any more. I'm leaving this note so when you come here to change you can read it, and after work you'll come and find me in bed and join me and we'll talk and talk and make love all night.

OK, Julia my darling? OK?

I'm not good at people being mad at me. I know, no one is, but I'm especially not. So don't be mad, OK?

And don't be jealous. I like him because he's your father, don't you know that? The more I find out about him, the more I know about you. I tried to tell you that, but you wouldn't listen, you told me that was all bullshit. It isn't, you know. When he talks about the past, or mentions your mother, there are times when, all of a sudden, I think that I'm you. Almost like making love, when you can't tell which is which any more. I want to be everywhere you were.

Bullshit, Elena, I hear you saying, such a load of crap.

OK, I like him. He's so much different from the people I grew up with, their flatness, their slyness, their hatred of anything exceptional. He's polite, and he knows so much, and he's careful to conceal how lonely he is, but he is, so lonely. In a way, it's like when I met you, crying your heart out over your mother, but not telling anybody. Too proud. You're alike that way. In some ways, you're more like him than you want to think. Oh you're different, and you're right, he's a bit pale sometimes, not grand and noisy like you, but there's the pride, the insistence on taking all the responsibility.

Do you know, I can't ever imagine your mother? Even when he talks about her. And I don't think that's all his fault. I know, you do. But she could have stood up on her hind legs, couldn't she?

I'm afraid that saying that will make you mad again. But we can't be beautiful lovers if we can't tell the truth. If we're going to travel to Africa and Europe together, we have to be able to say what we think.

Anyway, your mother's gone, and both of you are still suffering over it, and from the time I met him in the museum, I knew that I could give him something. He's talking about writing poems again. I got him moving. Just by being young and having an interesting face and Chinese hair. He doesn't really want any more than that, does he?

I'm trying to tell you this stuff as straight as I can so that from now on, there won't be any fights over it. Stupid, I guess, to try to avoid all the pains of the future, but you are so special to me that I want it to be only special between us. I want you to come here and find this on the table and just love me and come to bed and let me kiss you all over.

You think I'm fickle, don't you? Maybe I am, by your standards. You keep it all to yourself, and you hold it in tighter and tighter, and then you explode. And when somebody gets inside the wall you build around you, there's no room for anything else. I love that about you, the desperation, the feeling that I'm your only friend in a world of enemies. But I'm not like that. I see people, just strangers on the street, and I fall in love with them. I can't help that. I don't tell them. But that's the way the world takes me. Love, love, love. But then there's what I have with you, which is something else. That, as they say, is something else.

Does this make sense? Am I just getting in over my head? I'm trying to tell you the truth, my darling, that's part of how I love, trying to tell the truth.

A man in a restaurant, a sort of pirate look, flashing eyes and a dark beard, long legs in beautifully faded jeans, gold on his fingers and in his ear. Magic, I thought, and my heart did a little dance, a little old-fashioned Latin American dance, a tango maybe, and then I drank up my coffee and left, but he stayed in the mind.

Does it make me hateful, this fickleness, or whatever it is? Can't you just accept that it's a part of me? I see too much. I have all these little whimsies, but they don't change what I feel for you, under it all. I'm not simple and deep like you. I don't flow all one way. I skitter over things, like a dragon-fly.

You know how it was at art school. I was clever. I could always draw so quickly that you said I should be called E-line-a, not Elena, but when we got an assignment, you tore it to shreds, you really made something of it.

I'm going to do the drawings for your father. To make into a book. He needs that. I like his reticence, his stillness. I feel sorry for his loneliness. Don't be jealous. He's not my lover. You are.

Come to me in bed.

love love love love love
Elena

Arnold folded the letter and put it back in the book. Then he returned the book to the box, and carried the box into the bedroom where he put it on the floor of the clothes closet and pushed it to the back, using his foot to push it into the most distant, darkest corner. Now he would go to bed every night knowing that letter was within a few feet of where he lay. He could almost imagine that it might begin to glow in the

dark, the letters migrating from the page and writing
themselves on the ceiling over his bed. Each night he
could lie there and read the words in which he was
condescended to by Julia's lover.

He closed the closet door, went to the kitchen and
poured more whisky into a glass of ice.

What did she think she knew about Marie? Had he
said so much? Elena had found Julia crying her heart
out over her mother, when Arnold had never known
that she had done any such thing. While he flattered
himself that he saw the world from a wise distance,
penetrating its disguises, his own daughter was a
stranger to him. He had not guessed that she loved
women. Perhaps he mixed all his awareness with
water, for he hadn't the courage to take it straight.
Dear lost Marie: had she been elected to provide
excuses for his own fearfulness? The poems had
stopped, he supposed, when he had grown shy of
love and fear and metaphor, the way they caused the
world to grow slippery, one thing metamorphosed
into another, no defences. The first books had grown
from the shattering of his parents' marriage, from the
daily awareness of his mother's pain, the way the
glittering of her stripped nerves inhabited him. And
from Sandra, and all the confusions that exploded out
of what he had felt about her. It was a time when he
sometimes thought he might not survive, when fire,
water, earth and air were only alternate ways of
expressing anxiety, uncertainty, alarm, and the naked
music of that time was in his poems. Until he had
made himself into the man whose pride and reticence
and stillness Elena observed, a man who stood back
from life and called his distance wisdom, while he
spent his substance in the tuning of a wasted
sensibility.

He could hear again the voice of the letter, its gaiety, its determination to be pleased. He had never been able to offer gaiety—to Julia or to Marie, but now she was given it. It was what he had cared for in Elena, in his proud, stiff, foolish way. He was grateful that his reticence had kept him from pressing her further, to the place where she would have had to reject him openly. But why? Perhaps gaiety came with foolishness, and it was pride and care that closed its doors. He didn't know. What did he know? That he was a man standing alone in a room while outside it was snowing.

Daphne sat in a straight chair in the hospital waiting room. She had been getting into bed when the phone rang, Donald calling her from the outpatient department where they were patching him up after a car accident. To ask her to come and pick him up.

Until recently she hadn't minded going to bed alone, not knowing where her husband was; he always turned up before morning, half-crazy, needing to wake her and talk, or burrowing into her flesh like a hungry animal; but since that woman, Jeanie, all pretty and tearful, had arrived with her terrible story, Daphne had experienced a new kind of sick, fretful jealousy that gave her no peace. She'd been aware that Donald was unfaithful to her sometimes, but as long as he came home needing her to bring him back down to earth, always desperate to see her, to buy her things (though he never had the patience to wait until anything was bought, usually walked out of the store and waited, pacing, by the car), as long as he was attached to her, she'd lived with it. Once or twice, when she could tell by the look of him that he'd been screwing himself silly somewhere else, she'd felt a strong temptation to castrate him with a bread knife, but she held her peace.

It was different now. She had wanted a child so badly, and the knowledge that someone else had carried Donald's child, given birth to it, had undermined her, left her lost, and tonight, as she got ready for bed, not knowing where he was, she had been angry, all on edge. When the phone rang, she almost ran to it.

She looked across the waiting room, where a woman in a grey cloth coat, much the same nondescript colour as her hair, had fallen asleep, her head hanging to one side at an awkward angle. Daphne yawned. She had to go to work tomorrow, no matter how late she was tonight. Joan was out of town, and if Daphne didn't get there the store wouldn't open.

To one side of her, a young woman, her hair cheaply bleached, was cuddling a child, a boy, perhaps two years old, whose red feverish face had an unhealthy gloss, and whose eyes stared blindly. The thin hair at his temples was damp with sweat, and his mouth hung open to reveal tiny transparent teeth with spaces between. One of his hands rested at the side of his face as if he had been sucking his thumb, but no longer had the strength. Daphne could hear his breathing; almost, she thought, could feel the heat of his small body. The girl was wearing a red leather baseball jacket with the name Ron on one arm. Was Ron the father? Where was he now? Maybe he worked shifts. The face of the girl who held the sick child looked bored, angry, and Daphne wondered what she would do, if Daphne offered to take the child from her. For a thousand dollars, say. Right now, sick and feverish and only half conscious, red and ugly with illness, take the boy on her own lap, and when Donald

appeared, announce to him that this was his new son,
that she'd bought him for only a thousand dollars, a
good deal, really, as he must recognize.

A nurse came to the girl and helped her carry the
child through a glass door to the emergency rooms,
where the doctors would examine him. A doctor in a
white coat, an Indian with a neat moustache, came out
and woke the woman in the grey coat and began to
talk quietly to her.

The door opened again and Donald appeared, a
bandage on his forehead, his eyes shifting rapidly
around the room, as if searching for danger. He saw
Daphne, and his face changed, the wild unfocussed
look left it, and his legs propelled him quickly toward
her, and at that moment Daphne remembered how
her father had come to Toronto to see her when she
and Donald had become engaged, to warn her against
this man. Her kind, quiet father had found it hard to
put the words together, to explain that he was frightened for her.

"You been waiting long?" Donald said.

"Not long."

"Let's get the hell out of here."

Her dear sad father had been right that Donald was
an impossible man, but what he hadn't seen, and
couldn't see, was that her life would never be grey
like his own. Her father had embraced despair and
called it peace. Donald would never do that. He had
no gift for any kind of stillness. Right now he was
racing along two steps in front of her, his shoulders
hunched as if he were striding into a hurricane. In his
own way, she knew, he would have been a good
father, defending his children against the rest of the
world with the ferocity of an animal under attack. He
needed children to complete himself, though he didn't

know it. He believed it was no odds to him that she failed to get pregnant. But he'd had a child, even if it wasn't part of his life. A son. Who even unseen, had, until his early death, tied him to the earth while Daphne drifted, unattached. In quiet moments, staring out the window of the store when there were no customers, Daphne thought of the dead boy, Donald's son, found herself crying for him.

Donald was holding the glass door of the emergency ward open for her, and they went out into the cold air together.

"So what happened?" she said.

"I slid on the snow."

"Did they charge you?"

"With everything but contributing to the delinquency of a minor. And that was only because there wasn't a kid within blocks."

"How's the car?"

"A mess."

"Where did all this happen?"

"Out on Dovercourt."

"What were you doing out there in the middle of the night?"

"Cleaning that garage where Julia was renting. She left a box of stuff, so I took it to Arnold, and then I went back to clean up. Where's your car?"

"Down this street. So Julia's gone to Europe?"

"Someplace."

"On her own?"

"No. With some friend from art school."

They reached Daphne's little Toyota.

"You want to give me your keys?" Donald said.

"You can't drive."

"I don't like riding in a car when anyone else is driving."

"You're going to end up in jail."

"Just give me the keys, will you?"

Daphne handed him her keys and went round to the passenger door. Donald leaned across and opened it for her. He pulled out of the parking space and made a U-turn.

"I'm glad you were home when I called," Donald said.

"Where else would I be at that hour?"

"You never know."

"I've got no place else to be."

"You got the store."

Donald's driving was even jerkier and more erratic than usual. Daphne wondered if he might be in shock. He kept blinking his eyes, as if he couldn't see clearly.

"What would I be doing at the store at this time of night?"

"Screwing Sheldon Zemans."

Donald turned left, forcing the approaching car to brake quickly and cutting off a van that was just reaching the corner on the street they entered.

"I tell you what, Donald. You get me home without killing me or smashing up my car, and then take me to bed, and I'll tell you everything there is to know about Sheldon Zemans. If you'll tell me why you burned down that tattoo parlour."

"I don't think I want to know about Sheldon Zemans."

"Yes, you do. And I want to know about the tattoo parlour."

"What makes you think I burned it down?"

"You told me."

"I didn't."

"Not in so many words, but near enough."

Donald honked at the car dawdling in front of him,

pulled out to pass on the wrong side and raced through a yellow light.

"Did the doctor tell you you might be in shock?"

"He just put in the stitches and went on to the next guy."

"It hurt?"

"I got a headache."

They were close to home, and the closer they got, the faster he drove as if desperate to reach his goal. When they arrived at the house, he had braked, shut off the ignition and climbed out of the car before Daphne had her seat-belt undone. As she was getting out, he stopped on his way across the lawn and looked up toward the sky, which was clear and starry now, sucked in a big breath of cold air and went to open the front door.

"You want a Scotch?" he said once they were inside.

"A big one. Lots of ice. Will you bring it up?"

"Sure."

Daphne locked the front door and went up to the bedroom, where she undressed, revealing to herself the fat, drooping body that had humiliated her by its failure to conceive. Sometimes, when Donald was randy and light-hearted, she felt sumptuous, rich with treasure for him, but as often, she could not understand his desire for her fat body and wanted it to be hidden in darkness. Tonight she was outside her body, beyond it. The white thing she saw in the mirror was strange to her. She put the pillow behind her and pulled the covers over her, to wait, and within a few moments Donald arrived with the two drinks.

He passed one to her and put the other down on the table at his side of the bed, beside the lamp which he'd made out of a piece of driftwood at a summer camp thirty years before. He hated the lamp, but she insisted on keeping it.

"I need a hot shower," he said.

"I'll be here."

He took a drink of his Scotch and then disappeared down the hall.

She listened to the sounds, the door closing, the toilet flushing, then the humming of pipes, the muted splash of water hitting the sides of the shower stall. It was hypnotic, and her mind emptied, except that somewhere at the edge of her awareness was the image of that little boy, flaccid with illness, lying like a dead weight in his mother's arms. She should have made the offer, a thousand dollars, five thousand, anything, a million. She wanted that sick little boy for her own.

Donald appeared at the door, naked, his thick muscular body reddened by the hot water. He'd put on a little weight over the years, but evenly over his whole body, a little thickening of the waist, an accumulation over the kidneys, but not enough to alter the shape, not the way hers had been altered. His hair stood on end from being rubbed dry with a towel, and his body hair stood out from the skin. He came to the bed and drank and then climbed in beside her, bent and rubbed his lips over her breast. She could feel the roughness of the whiskers that had grown since morning.

"So tell me about Sheldon," he said, drawing back. "Is he hung like a stallion?"

"I have no idea."

"You said you were going to tell me everything there is to know."

"Sheldon's gay, Donald."

"Sheldon's a poof?"

"Poof, faggot, queer, fairy, fruit, whatever you want to call it."

"He's married, isn't he?"

"Yes. Three children."

"So how do you know he's queer?"

"He told me."

"It's probably part of his technique. Make you feel sorry for him. So you'll take him to bed to straighten him out."

"Donald, you're stubborn and stupid sometimes. The man is miserable. He's madly in love with some young guy who's a night clerk in a hotel. Sheldon goes round to the hotel every afternoon, and his friend arranges to get them a free room, and afterward he showers and goes home to his wife. It's awful. He hates it. Can't you understand that?"

"Why did he tell you?"

"I don't know. Maybe I have a sympathetic face."

Donald looked over at her, as if he might be studying her face to see if that was true.

"So he's not hustling you."

"I think I'm the only person he's told. He's in terrible shape, spending a fortune on this boy in the hotel, buying him presents, going on trips with him that are supposed to be business trips."

"Why doesn't he just tell his wife?"

"Why didn't you ever tell me why you burned down the tattoo parlour?"

There was a stiff silence, and Daphne could hear his breathing change. She felt as if the air in the room had grown thin, as if all the oxygen had gone out of it.

"So Sheldon's that way," he said, in a strange distant kind of voice. "In love with a fruity desk clerk."

Daphne waited. She wasn't going to ask again. It would be humiliating to ask again.

"Yes. I burned it down," he said.

Daphne waited.

"I had to get rid of the Rat," he said.

She didn't know what he was talking about. It was a joke and she had missed the point.

"What rat?"

"She lived upstairs. She got under my skin. I don't know why. Nothing special about her. Buck teeth, skinny. You're right in a way, what you said when you were smashing all that Doulton, I've cheated now and then, but it honestly never mattered. A meal away from home, that's all. But this one, she got under my skin. I had to get her out of there."

"Why didn't you just tell her to move out?"

"She wouldn't go."

"Was she in love with you?"

"Why would she be?"

"You're an attractive man."

"Glad you think so."

"Probably she was in love with you. She couldn't bear to leave."

"No. She'd fuck anything that moved."

"Then why wouldn't she leave?"

"I don't know."

"Do you miss her?"

"Not much."

He didn't speak for a few seconds.

"Probably not much," he said.

Daphne took a drink, but she couldn't seem to taste the Scotch, and then when it was in her mouth, it wouldn't quite go down her throat.

"Why did you have to get rid of her?" she said. "So badly that you burned the place and sold it so cheap."

"You know why."

"Tell me."

"I swore I wouldn't do that. Be like my old man. Marry one woman and then decide I couldn't get along without a different one."

They sat, side by side, silent, like two pieces of sculpture.

"I'm not the greatest husband in the world, Daph, but I give it a shot."

Daphne put down her glass and reached across under the covers. She put her hand between his thighs and took hold of his testicles. The little elliptical balls rolled loosely between her fingers under the skin, and she squeezed, hard.

"Jesus, Daph," he shouted, his face suddenly wild, with that expression it took on sometimes and you never knew whether he might explode and destroy something.

"Cut it out," he said. "You're not supposed to do that."

"Why not?" she said. "The damn balls were no good to me. They wouldn't make me a baby." She squeezed again.

"Cut it out."

"Why wouldn't they make me a baby?"

"I don't know."

"There was one at the hospital, a little boy, sick, and his mother looked tired and crabby. I was thinking I could offer to buy him. A thousand dollars cash. She looked like she might take it."

"They wouldn't let her do that."

"Who knows? They have surrogate mothers. You hire some girl to have the baby."

"So you want me to jerk off in a doctor's office, and they put it inside a stranger and then we get the kid?"

"It's an idea. Or we could adopt one."

"You never know what you might get."

"That's true even when you have your own."

She was stroking him gently now, and his voice had lost some of its edge. It was nice, in a way magical, that she could calm him, draw him down into some kind of rest. He was pulling all the covers off her, touching her with his fingers, looking at her.

"Fat old body," she said.

"You want me to turn the lights out?"

"No. Leave them on."